Season by Season

SIGNS AND PORTENTS

The *Babylon 5* Library
from Del Rey Books

Babylon 5: *In the Beginning*

Creating Babylon 5

Season by Season Guides

Signs and Portents

The Coming of Shadows

Point of No Return

No Surrender, No Retreat

Babylon 5 *Security Manual*

Season by Season

SIGNS AND PORTENTS

Jane Killick

The Ballantine Publishing Group

New York

A Del Rey® Book
Published by The Ballantine Publishing Group

TM & Copyright © 1997, 1998 by Warner Bros.

http://www.randomhouse.com/delrey/
http://www.thestation.com

Library of Congress Catalog Card Number: 97-97204
ISBN: 0-345-42447-6

Contents

Acknowledgments   vii

Foreword   ix

Getting **Babylon 5** into Orbit   1

Babylon 5's First Season   13

Signs and Portents: Episode Guide   25
    Pilot: "The Gathering"   27
    1 "Midnight on the Firing Line"   34
    2 "Soul Hunter"   41
    3 "Born to the Purple"   47
    4 "Infection"   53
    5 "The Parliament of Dreams"   59
    6 "Mind War"   66
    7 "The War Prayer"   72
    8 "And the Sky Full of Stars"   79
    9 "Deathwalker"   86
    10 "Believers"   93
    11 "Survivors"   99
    12 "By Any Means Necessary"   106
    13 "Signs and Portents"   113
    14 "TKO"   119
    15 "Grail"   125
    16 "Eyes"   131
    17 "Legacies"   138
    18 "A Voice in the Wilderness, Part One"   144
    19 "A Voice in the Wilderness, Part Two"   150
    20 "Babylon Squared"   157
    21 "The Quality of Mercy"   164
    22 "Chrysalis"   170

Acknowledgments

This book would not have been possible without all of the wonderful people who gave generously of their time and their comments to make it as comprehensive as it is. I would like to thank them and all the behind-the-scenes people at *Babylon 5* who were so helpful when I was doing my research, especially the heroic Joanne Higgins, who should be elevated to sainthood! Thanks also to Brian Cooney for arranging the Michael O'Hare interview, and to Sandra Bruckner for arranging the foreword.

On a personal note, I would like to thank Liz Holliday and Chris O'Shea for being friends. And a special thank you to David Bassom.

Foreword

Working on *Babylon 5* was quite an experience. Although I have worked on Broadway, in movies, and in TV, this was my first full-time TV series and my first venture into science fiction. What little I knew about the genre when I began the show, I learned from my son, Ben. For years he'd taken me into comic-book shops and bookstores, looking for all the items children collect—books, cards, caps, etc. What I discovered on *Babylon 5*, however, was quite different.

Working in TV is not all that dissimilar to working on stage. You follow the instructions of the director, learn your lines, hit your mark, and do the best job you can with the material. You try to discover who the character is that you are portraying and make that character come to life, for you and the audience. With *Babylon 5*, however, computer graphics are a large part of the overall production. While standing in front of a blue screen, you must use your imagination to "see" the creature in "Grail," the massive machine on Epsilon 3 in "A Voice In the Wilderness," and the destruction of Babylon 5 in "Babylon Squared." You can get some idea of the image from the director, but it's still very much up to you to make the scene believable.

During that first year of *Babylon 5*, I was fortunate to work with some truly talented people—including David Warner in "Grail," Theodore Bikel in "TKO," and Morgan Sheppard in "Soul Hunter." They were generous with their insights and advice about the acting profession.

I learned a lot while working on *Babylon 5*. Joe Straczynski has put together a wonderful story, and working with people like John Flinn, Mira Furlan, Richard Biggs, and Bill Mumy made the experience a very enjoyable one. When I returned to the set to make "War Without End," the cast made me feel right at home, and I very much enjoyed working with Bruce Boxleitner.

My favorite episodes are "By Any Means Necessary," "Babylon Squared," and "And the Sky Full of Stars." I like these episodes not only because I had a lot to do in them, but also because each had a significant part to play in the overall story. While "By Any Means Necessary" is not truly an arc story, it gives you a lot of insight into the character of Commander Sinclair.

Going back to *Babylon 5* for "War Without End" last year was somewhat like completing a journey—Sinclair's return from Minbar, taking Babylon 4 back in time to fight the Shadows, transforming into Valen. Joe Straczynski has worked very hard to tell this story, and I am happy to have been a part of it.

Michael O'Hare
(Commander Sinclair)

Getting Babylon 5 into Orbit

From the moment J. Michael Straczynski presented the idea for *Babylon 5* in front of his fellow producers in 1987, it created a lot of excitement. All of them saw an opportunity to do something new and different in science fiction terms and set about the task of persuading others to put their weight behind the idea. But it wasn't until 1992 that they finally succeeded in getting the pilot made. It was a long and arduous process that has a five-year story arc all its own.

Joe Straczynski got to know *Babylon 5* producers Douglas Netter and John Copeland while they were working together on a troubled children's series called *Captain Power and the Soldiers of the Future*. It was, shall we say, not the most sophisticated science fiction show in the world and was beset by production problems, not least because of the involvement of the toy manufacturer Mattel, who was using it as promotion for a range of toys. *Babylon 5*, Straczynski insisted, could be different.

"Joe brought this project to Doug and myself and said 'Science fiction really doesn't have to be the way that it appeared on *Captain Power*,' " John Copeland remembers. "He'd come up with this idea which was extremely character driven; it was not a hardware show. It was contained in that it was not a show that visited new planets and new groups of aliens every week, so theoretically you could create a production model that you could do on a budget."

The idea that *Babylon 5* could explore the wonders of the universe from one space station was the masterstroke that made the project affordable. For Executive Producer Doug Netter, it was the key to selling the show. "When I read *Babylon 5* not only did I like the project and the premise and the characters, but it became apparent that Joe had done exactly what he said he was going to do, which was write a project that could be contained and could be produced for television at a budget that everybody could live with."

The next stage was to commission artist Peter Ledger to produce some conceptual designs to help visualize some of the ideas in Joe Straczynski's head. "Most TV executives are frightened of science fiction and wouldn't understand it on a bet," says Joe disparagingly. "They had to be educated to what a space station of this magnitude would involve. Most of them, when they think about a space station, think about [the real Russian space station] Mir. They don't understand what it actually is. You say five miles long, and they can't conceive of it. So we thought nice friendly pictures would help them."

Armed with some pretty pictures, a pilot script, a breakdown of where the story could go, a model of how it could be produced on a budget, and bags of enthusiasm, they went knocking on doors. And that's when the problems started. They approached a host of networks and syndication companies, including CBS, HBO, ABC, and Fox, with no success.

"I think that after making the rounds of the three major networks at that time, we realized that science fiction had a bad reputation," says John Copeland. "It was from the wrong side of the tracks, as it were. People would always say 'Oh, we can do this on a budget, we can do this on a schedule,' and then always proceeded to do otherwise. Everyone will lie incredibly in Hollywood in order to get a show made. So even though we were very earnest in saying 'No, we can do this; we've studied for this test,' nobody believed us because nobody had done it before."

The general perception was: nobody watches science fiction apart from the fans. And, in many respects, they were right. The history of the genre is peppered with shows that were hideously expensive, derided by the critics, and a disaster in the all-important ratings war. For most TV executives, it was simply too much of a risk.

"What studios and networks have liked in the past are science fiction shows that aren't science fiction shows," John explains. "Like *Quantum Leap*. It has ten seconds [of science fiction] at the beginning and ten seconds at the end, and the rest of it is kind of an ordinary drama. They liked shows that felt that way, that were comfortable. The problem also with a lot of the stuff that has been done is they've thought, 'Oh, it's science fiction, we can do whatever we want, it doesn't have to make sense, it doesn't have to be logical.' But you'll find that the majority of people who read science fiction and fantasy on a regular basis are extremely well educated. Even if they had not had the benefit to go on to college or graduate school, they are thinkers and they make you toe the line on storytelling a lot stronger than people who are into other types of material. I think they're very demanding as an audience, and that's something for the longest time I just don't think studio and network executives got."

It didn't matter how brilliant the idea was, how enthusiastic the production team was, how detailed their production model was, and how many millions of dollars science fiction films like *Star Wars* and *ET* had made at the box office, most television executives had no interest in a project like *Babylon 5*. A lot of them had had bad experiences with science fiction in the past, and they didn't want to go through it all again. Merely mentioning the term *science fiction* put people off. "[They thought] the broad general audience that loves to sit down with a Coke or a beer and watch the show couldn't be reached by science fiction," says Doug Netter. "Many station owners and marketing people believed that science fiction appealed to only a limited audience and that it couldn't break out or cross over into a more general audience. Since they knew it was the most expensive kind of production you could do, they felt that they were into a situation of too much money and too small a market. They didn't want to take the chance and preferred more conventional programming. They said it to us time and time again, and that was the roadblock we constantly ran into."

In order to circumnavigate that problem, the three producers came up with a strategy to convince the men in suits that science fiction *could* have mass appeal and that *Babylon 5* would be the show to do it. As John Copeland remembers: "The way that it was always pitched was, 'You know, back when television was starting in the late forties and the early fifties, cop shows were not popular because they thought that crime dramas appealed to a very narrow spectrum of people. Then came *Dragnet* [starring] Jack Webb, and it dealt with true stories and the guys were like real human beings. They had lives outside of their jobs, and they talked about getting indigestion at the barbecue and things like that. People crossed over; they got into it because it was the depiction of the characters [that interested them].' That's what was used in describing what *Babylon 5* was like. It was a *Hill Street Blues* in space—it was a drama about characters that happened to be set in space. It wasn't a show that was about spaceships; it wasn't a show that was about space battles. Sure, those elements entered into it, but it was about the characters and had the potential to appeal to a broader viewer base."

Star Trek was the perfect example of that. Twenty years since it was originally shown, it was still popular in reruns; it had spawned a plethora of spin-off movies, which were making money; and a new series, *Star Trek: The Next Generation*, was in production. It, therefore, proved that science fiction could command a large audience. "No, *Star Trek* is its own unique phenomenon," John Copeland remembers being told over and over again. "It's not equatable to anything else; there's just no interest in science fiction."

So instead of being a help to *Babylon 5*, *Star Trek* became a hindrance. "There were many who believed that there was only room in the television market for one science fiction television series, *Star Trek*," says Doug Netter. "We didn't believe that. We thought there could be as many science fiction shows as there were cop shows or hospital shows."

The specter of *Star Trek* continued to haunt them as they went from one network to another. Joe Straczynski offers an explanation as to why. "If you look back at the history of American television, there has not been any other space-based science fiction series that's gone beyond three seasons until *Babylon 5* came along," he says. "In addition, the general sense in Hollywood is there's not an audience for science fiction: there's only an audience for *Star Trek*; that if there truly were an audience for SF, *Star Trek* would have bred more science fiction shows. In reality that doesn't happen. *Trek* breeds more *Trek*—it doesn't breed more SF."

Joe Straczynski pitched the whole five-year arc to a succession of faceless TV moguls, usually falling back on the hook line of "*Casablanca* in space" to get his concept across. But there was just no getting through to some people. There was one pitch to a network in which it became clear to him halfway through that he had lost the battle. "I showed them a painting of the interior of the station which is the garden area [showing that] the station rotates to create gravity," says Joe. "The guy looked at somebody standing on what would normally be the ceiling point of view and said 'What keeps him up there?' Stupidly, I said, 'Krazy Glue!' He said, 'Well, that won't work. He can't move around. He can't interact with other actors!' "

By this time they needed a break, and they got it through a man called Evan Thompson of a station group called Chris Craft, later to become United Television. Doug Netter told him about *Babylon 5* in true Hollywood tradition over lunch, and then followed it up by sending over the pilot script. "When we saw the script, that's when we first got very enthusiastic about it," says Evan Thompson. "We hear a lot of ideas for television shows, read a lot of scripts, and very few of them strike a responsive chord with us. But we thought this was a terrific script; it was a terrific idea; it was different from anything that had really been on television before. It was a true, in our mind anyway, 'science fiction' television show, and it would have integrity with those loyal science fiction addicts.

"But beyond that we thought it had much broader appeal," he continues. "The story was just a good story, the characters were really creative and fresh, and we thought that the *Babylon 5* team was very collaborative and very friendly, and we thought it was just a very attractive vehicle."

Some other people who had looked at the project had been frightened by the concept of a five-year story arc. They thought it was a surefire way to alienate the audience, who would feel lost if they missed an episode. That wasn't the case with Evan Thompson. "It demonstrated to us that Joe had a plan, and he really had thought the project through," he says. "He was flexible of where the story could go, but he had a pretty good idea of where it was all headed, and to us that was pretty important. [It was], at least, unusual because a lot of people come in with an idea for the first episode and after that, God knows what the show's going to be! He had such a clear idea of what the show was and where it was headed and that was very intriguing to us. I don't think we've ever seen anything that has been that thorough in its presentation or that long-ranging. We see some shows, particularly soap operas, where bibles are written that show you what might happen with a story six or nine months into the series, but nothing that goes for four or five years."

It was Evan Thompson who decided to face the *Star Trek* problem head-on and take the project to the people who make *Star Trek*, Paramount. They knew about science fiction; they knew it could generate a sizable audience, and if anyone would see the value in the show, it would be them. But they ran up against the age-old problem of money. The *Babylon 5* producers claimed they could make a space drama for half the budget of *Star Trek: The Next Generation*, and the people behind *Star Trek* didn't believe it could be done. So, after Paramount sat on the idea for nine months without doing anything with it, Evan Thompson asked for the script back. "But I was encouraged because the people I knew over at Paramount liked it, so to me what they were concerned about—which was how much it was going to cost to make—I was not concerned about. The bigger concern to me was, could it make a good television show? And they sort of endorsed the fact that it could."

The next port of call was Warner Bros. United Television had worked with them before on other projects so Evan Thompson was able to take it straight to the president of Warner Bros. Domestic Television Distribution, Dick Robertson. That's where the show found its second champion.

"From a business point of view, we always liked the idea of a space science fiction show," says Dick Robertson. "Primarily because it tends to reach a very young and affluent demographic, usually young men, which is a very difficult audience to get on TV. The genre had always interested us, but we never really had seen a specific project that got us all excited until Doug and Joe and John Copeland brought in *Babylon 5*."

. One of the most important factors behind securing the support of Evan Thompson and Dick Robertson was Doug Netter. His reputation was, in many ways, more important than the ideas behind the show. *Babylon 5* may have been a revolutionary idea for a science fiction television drama, but for the men who would have to put their money on the table, the revolutionary production plan made all the difference. "I've known Doug Netter for years, and he's a dear friend of mine," says Dick Robertson. "We knew what Doug could do; we knew he was a man of his word. If he said he was going to do something, you could pretty much count on him delivering, and in the world of Hollywood, that's not always the case. Doug is a guy that we had great faith in. He's one of the better producers in the city, and he brings programs in on budget, he brings them in on time, and he gets along well with his cast members and people both in front of the camera and behind the camera. He's just really a good man, and we love doing business with him."

"I had seen him from way back," says Evan. "He produced a couple of miniseries, the names of which I don't even remember anymore, for Metro Media. Then I followed him when he did a show for Disney down in Australia, which I thought was quite good. So I'd known Doug for a long time and knew about his production capabilities. I sincerely believed that he could produce programming less expensively than most people in Hollywood. More than that, when he said he could do something for a budget, he actually delivered on that budget. So I actually thought he was a very responsible producer in Hollywood based upon what I had known. Joe I did not know as well. I knew of him; at the time he was writing for *Murder, She Wrote*, which was another successful television show, but in his case, quite frankly, I thought his work product spoke for itself. He wrote a very good initial script, which is what kept our interest for all the time that we were trying to get the show on the air."

With one foot in the door at Warner Bros. and another at United Television, work began on securing a deal to make the show. "He [Dick Robertson] is really an experienced marketer," says Evan Thompson. "He started to get involved in how we could finance the show. We had conversations with a number of international entities, some of which Doug had relationships with and he brought into the picture, and others came from Warner Bros. And there was one Italian group that I brought in. I think we probably spent over a year trying to make that come together, having meetings with various people who happened to be in the country at the time or waiting for them to come into the country to have a meeting with them."

Eventually, interest was secured from the German station NDR and from Mitsubishi. They agreed in principle, along with Warner Bros. and United Television, to put up a quarter of the money each. It would then be syndicated across the United States, and sold to Europe through NDR and to the Far East through Mitsubishi. "Putting the deal together was a monumental task," says Doug Netter. "It's hard enough with one, but now when you get to four partners, you get an exponential ratio of difficulty."

As Doug Netter was struggling to get the various parties to sign on the dotted line, Warner Bros. was putting together the Prime Time Entertainment Network (PTEN). This is a network of about a hundred local television stations in the States, headed by United Television. It gave them access to a powerful body that could syndicate Babylon 5 across America at a stroke. So, as Evan Thompson remembers, they abandoned the international deal in favor of PTEN: "We finally said 'To heck with them all—we will bear the risk of financing the show ourselves.' "

That commitment took a long time to achieve. There were still great doubts over whether Babylon 5 could really be produced for the price its producers claimed. Their business plan was very simple. It said a lot of money could be saved if people made efforts to plan ahead, if the action was mostly contained in the space station, and, most important, if they took a new approach to the way they achieved the special effects. "Warner Bros. was afraid because of their experience with *V*, the TV series," remembers John Copeland. "At the time that they did *V* [a series about an alien invasion of Earth], they were still forced to do all of their visual effects as full-screen opticals. So here they are, they're doing a TV show and yet they're having to use the same film optical processes as *2001* and *Star Wars*! That's an incredibly inefficient way to spend your money, because your end product is going to end up on a television screen. There's a big difference between that and a thirty-foot screen that you see when you go to the cinema. But there was the Warner Bros. experience with *V* we had to get over, with *Max Headroom* and, more recently than both of those, *The Flash*. We met with Steve Papazian, who was the head of production for Warner Bros. at the time, and sat and talked to him about what we were going to do and what technology we were going to employ. Steve had been the production manager on *V*, and he turned around and said, 'Well these guys are absolutely right, because in the succeeding ten years that have gone down the road from where we were at *V*, there is all of this new stuff that you can use in television that you could not do before.' "

That meant computer-generated imagery (CGI), a process that is essential to creating the illusion of Babylon 5 in space. Every space scene—from Babylon 5 spinning above Epsilon 3 to the starfuries and the battles—are created inside a computer. "If Joe had come along with this ten years earlier, it would not have been possible to do *Babylon 5* the way that we do," says John. "We have taken advantage of the technological and digital revolution in spades, embraced it in a way that I don't believe anyone else has done as successfully as we have in television production today."

At the time, of course, it was all unproven technology as far as TV was concerned. It seemed that the only way to convince the skeptical TV executives was to give them a demonstration, and that's where special-effects wizard Ron Thornton came in. "At the time Ron had an Amiga [computer] and was messing around with it," remembers John. "He kind of had an epiphany about what this thing could do. The 'video toaster' that he had plugged into his Amiga—the lightwave 3D—had been designed by Alan Hastings. All Alan really wanted to do was to make spaceships. This animation package kind of came along and landed in our laps at the right time. This was something that allowed us to do some test renderings and to show people what our effects would look like on the budget. No one had really done that before, and there were folks in the production community who thought we were Looney Tunes. It's kind of appropriate that we landed up in Warner Bros. for that very reason."

Ron Thornton produced a thirty-second clip of animation to show exactly what could be achieved. Doug Netter, John Copeland, and Joe Straczynski then took it to Warner Bros. and the PTEN consortium for a make-or-break presentation. It is an experience Joe is unlikely to forget. "When we went in to pitch the show to PTEN it was going to be us and two or three Warner Bros. shows," he says. "Warners is like a series of competing fiefdoms: there isn't one thing called 'Warner Bros.,' there are a lot of different divisions. And division B heard that division A was doing a network and so [they thought], 'We should get all of our shows in there.' So they went from three or four shows to about fourteen shows being pitched.

"We asked them what we should do to prepare for this big meeting. It was us and the executive committee of PTEN, which is about fifteen or eighteen very important station guys across the country. [We said], 'Shall we bring souvenirs—hats, T-shirts, mugs, bumper stickers—to give to the guys?' We were told, 'No, don't bother; just bring the thirty-second CGI clip and Joe to tell the story.' Well, we show up on the first day and all the other shows are there—they've got music videos, they've got caps, they've got T-shirts, and they've got bumper stickers and all this stuff. We've got thirty seconds of animation and me—and I'm nothing to write home about!

"So another show is pitching before us in the main room, and Doug and I are waiting in the back to go in for our first of two meetings," Joe continues. "As we're pacing back and forth, I'm pissed off about all this and worried about it and grinding my teeth, and I hear a crack. I had split a molar lengthwise. I opened my mouth, and the cold air-conditioned air raced in—I saw colors I never saw before! And Doug looked at me and said, 'We should have this taken care of, and we should come back tomorrow to do this,' and I said, 'No, by tomorrow they will have heard ten stories, and they will be glazed over, and we won't have a chance, so we have to do this now.' "

"Joe's pretty cool and I'm pretty cool when it comes to those kinds of things," says Doug. "We couldn't believe after we waited all this time and we were getting ready to make a big presentation, Joe had broken his tooth. He had no time to go and have it fixed. So there we were."

"I got a big tumbler of ice water," says Joe, "a lot of ice, sucked it back, held it for about ten minutes and the tears ran down my face, until I couldn't feel the pain anymore. We went in and we pitched it . . . Pitching to these guys is like singing in front of a painting: there really isn't a whole lot of reaction. I left the room thinking I had completely screwed it up, and they weren't going to give us the order."

But it hadn't been screwed up. The CGI clip had tipped the scales in their favor. With the added endorsement of Steve Papazian, who had studied and validated their budget, schedule, and unique approach to special effects, they were on their way. It took a couple more meetings, at which the producers were joined by Ron Thornton and designer John Iacovelli, but eventually they came away with a commitment to produce a pilot.

"We were a little disappointed," admits Doug Netter, "because we thought we would get an order for twenty-two episodes. But we didn't, and it worked out just as well. We did the pilot, which was enormously successful, and it was done on budget, on schedule, and everybody was agreed that the quality was there, that we had made it work. So we proved our point."

So ended five years of struggle. An order for a full season of twenty-two episodes followed, and at last *Babylon 5* was in orbit. In the intervening time they had faced rejection upon rejection, but they never gave up. "One of the things that I learned from Doug is that the projects you really passionately believe in, you don't give up on," concludes John Copeland. "It may take you a long time to get it off the ground, but you just don't give up. You persevere. Joe felt that way about it, Doug and I felt that way about it, and it took a long time to get some other people to believe in that."

"If it hadn't been for Joe's passion, Dick Robertson's marketing expertise, and Doug's ability to produce quality programming for less than normal amounts of money, I don't think the show would have ever gotten on the air," says Evan Thompson. "But it did. All of us seemed to stick together. It became a mission: we became advocates of the show and just wanted to get it on the air to prove that we were right."

Babylon 5's First Season

When *Babylon 5* first appeared in 1993, it presented a vision that had never been attempted before. Science fiction had been drama's poor relation in television for many years, with the genre's occasional examples of brilliance overshadowed by the mass of unintelligent escapist entertainment shows. *Babylon 5* was different: it wanted to take the richness of science fiction literature and transplant it to the screen. It wanted to tell a story that progressed with each episode, where things that happened one week were not simply forgotten the next, where actions had consequences. It didn't always succeed, but the vision was always there in a form powerful enough to break the mold of science fiction television in the nineties.

Babylon 5 is a story told on an epic scale, and the first season is very much about establishing the background against which the saga will unfold. It is about introducing the aliens, their cultures, and their conflicts. It is about explaining Humanity's position in space, its relationship with the aliens, and its political system. It is about familiarizing the audience with some of the elements that will become more significant later on. It is about getting to know the characters, their hopes, their fears, their failures, and their potential.

At the same time it is also about telling good stories. The first season makes an effort to be kind to its audience. *Babylon 5*'s renowned story arc is less visible in these earlier episodes, the show instead preferring to draw in casual viewers with good stories that will encourage them to tune in again. The show tries not to overburden the viewer with background information, but rather allows it to filter through while the main story continues in the foreground. Sometimes the background information actually becomes the story, as with "A Voice in the Wilderness," in which the audience discovers the Great Machine of Epsilon 3 at the same time as the characters.

But it would be fair to say the series took a while to get into its stride in terms of storytelling, most notably in the pilot. When you look back on it with the benefit of hindsight, it is amazing how much background and story arc was laid down that early on. G'Kar explains that there are no Narn telepaths; Garibaldi talks to Londo about Earth's first contact with an alien race; Delenn is angered when G'Kar vilifies the Grey Council; Sinclair recounts his experiences in the Battle of the Line; G'Kar mentions how Narn was invaded by the Centauri; and so forth. Some of this was necessary, but the weight of the exposition was such that it ended up slowing down the story. The pilot is basically about Sinclair being framed for the attempted assassination of Ambassador Kosh, but Lyta Alexander doesn't point the finger at Sinclair until forty-seven minutes in.

The first episode, "Midnight on the Firing Line," is, in many respects, a second pilot that reintroduces the characters and the world, with a little more action and a little more characterization. Sinclair is given some heroics to do by chasing after Raiders, and the character moments are in part represented by Ivanova talking about the death of her mother and Garibaldi's bizarre session in front of the *Duck Dodgers* cartoon with Delenn. The focus of the plot, however, is the Narn invasion of the Centauri colony Ragesh 3. It sets up the central conflict between G'Kar and Londo, but it doesn't work as well as it might because their argument is across a negotiating table. An effort is made to personalize it for Londo through his nephew on Ragesh 3, but it doesn't solve the problem that the invasion happens off screen. In a way similar to "Infection" later on (when we are asked to care about a race of extinct aliens that we have not met and have not seen), it doesn't fully engage the characters in the action.

Things start to come together in "Soul Hunter" with a plot that does everything you could ask of it. First of all, it fully engages the characters by putting Delenn in a life-threatening situation and pitting Sinclair against the alien

who threatens her life. Moreover, it has a strong and intriguing science fiction idea at its heart, which it explores
from every angle. Lots of background and arc information
is slipped in, but it is done with a deft hand, adding to rather than detracting from the story. If you had never seen
Babylon 5 before and had no intention of ever watching it
again, you could quite happily sit down and enjoy "Soul
Hunter" as a story in its own right.

That is what Babylon 5 was mostly aiming to do in the first
year and continued to do so with a string of other good stories. "The Parliament of Dreams" is peppered with several
intriguing subplots and driven by the main plot of the death
threat against G'Kar. In "Mind War," Talia's former lover puts
the station at risk with his escalating telekinetic powers. "And
the Sky Full of Stars" excels with Sinclair forced to relive his
experiences at the Battle of the Line. "Believers" is a particularly strong stand-alone episode with its powerful depiction
of what happens to an innocent child when two ideologies
clash. "Survivors" is a strong character piece for Garibaldi,
showing him as a man with a troubled past who can fall off
the wagon at any time. The dock strike in "By Any Means
Necessary" highlights Babylon 5's uncompromising stance
on realism. "TKO" is a great turn for Ivanova as she is forced
to face her feelings about the death of her father. "Babylon
Squared" is one of the best episodes of the season for the
way it uses the characters, time travel, and action to set up
one of the show's main mysteries. "The Quality of Mercy"
must also make the list of good stories for the way it com-
bines the fun of Londo and Lennier with a crazed killer and a
disgraced doctor trying to rediscover her life.

Some episodes were less successful. "The War Prayer"
fails because it has too many subplots competing for space.
"TKO" has a rather uninteresting boxing plot (giving it the
honor of appearing in both lists). "A Voice in the Wilderness"
also makes the disappointing list because, despite some
great moments, the story doesn't quite stretch over two
parts.

There is a dark thread that runs through Babylon 5, and
this is set up beautifully by the first season. It has a gritty

realism that reflects many of the unpleasant aspects of the real world, ever present in Down-Below, a dark and dismal area of the station where the destitute live. It occasionally comes to prominence in the plots, but most of the time it is portrayed as an accepted part of Babylon 5, a constant reminder that this is a world that hasn't solved all of Humanity's problems.

The gritty realism is perhaps best highlighted in "By Any Means Necessary," in which the station is crippled by a dock strike. Here is the reality of the space station, the grassroots, blue-collar workers who keep everything running, suffering the same problems as workers experience in the modern world. This is a future that acknowledges that space travel is expensive, that budgets are tight, that cutbacks and corner-cutting exist just as they have always done. As Sinclair is thrust into the middle of an industrial-relations dispute, he experiences one of the truths that keep recurring in *Babylon 5*, that there are no easy answers. Sinclair solves the problem only by going against the wishes of the Earth Senate, a decision that avoids immediate repercussions only because of the public support for his stance.

That is taken a stage further in "Believers," which presents a dilemma that cannot be solved. When the characters are faced with a choice between performing surgery on a child and violating his religion, and abiding by his religion and allowing him to die, they discover there is no right answer. *Babylon 5* makes no compromises on that storyline. Dr. Franklin performs the operation and the boy recovers, but because of their religion, the parents kill the child. It is a tragic but inevitable ending.

Babylon 5's philosophy is that life, like people, is flawed. The characters, particularly the Humans, have traumas in their past, problems in their present, or internal scars that give them an edge. Sinclair, as J. Michael Straczynski says elsewhere in this book, is a wounded bird, a man who, as Delenn comments in "A Voice in the Wilderness," is "searching for a purpose." Garibaldi is an ex-alcoholic with a history of being thrown out of jobs because of his abuse of the bottle. And Ivanova is a woman who has lost her brother in the war and her telepathic mother through suicide; she hides her feelings behind duty.

The telepathic thread is a part of the *Babylon 5* world that really caught the imagination in the first year and played a significant part in many of the episodes. Psi powers have a long tradition in science fiction, although, prior to *Babylon 5*, they were treated as a fun thing to have by most television SF. Here, telepaths are something to be controlled and, in some instances, feared. If you are Human, being a telepath means constantly hearing the voices of other minds, having to wear gloves to minimize physical contact, and having to operate within strict Psi Corps rules. The horror of the Psi Corps is first expressed in Ivanova's speech to Talia Winters in "Midnight on the Firing Line," when she describes what happened to her mother, and is emphasized with the arrival of Bester the Psi Cop in "Mind War."

The power is not ever seen as a gift but more of an affliction. In "The Quality of Mercy," Talia has to suffer the horrors of a serial killer's mind as part of her role in the Psi Corps. In "Eyes," Mr. Gray, a military specialist with the Corps, describes how the surfacing of his talent effectively ended his chosen career. Individual telepaths, with the possible exception of Bester in the first season, are seen as sympathetic characters. The organization they are forced to belong to is not. The concept of this incredible talent that has become something to be feared is intriguing to many people. "Mind War" sets up the contradiction quite simply. It may be a beautiful thing when two telepaths make love, but it can also be a horrific thing when a telepath deep scans another.

"Mind War" is central to this thread and sets up a lot of things for later on. While the telepaths come to prove their use in the Shadow War, the arrival of Jason Ironheart allows a closer look into the workings of the Psi Corps. He reveals that the Psi Corps is only interested in control and not just control over telepaths but over economics and politics, too.

The political background is probably the most subtle yet one of the more important threads to be set up in the first year. Babylon 5 is not a separate entity: it is an Earth-run station affected by the shifting politics on Earth. Throughout the season nuggets of information are slipped in, mostly from Interstellar News Network. For the casual viewer, these act as little color pieces, giving depth to the Babylon 5 universe by talking about things happening off the station. But for people watching closely, they build up a picture of the larger events that actually shape Babylon 5. The first episode, "Midnight on the Firing Line," has a tiny subplot about the presidential election on Earth, which is resolved at the end with the election of Luis Santiago. As the season progresses we hear little bits and pieces about Santiago's policies to maintain relations with alien governments, most notably in "Survivors," in which we hear of his support for Babylon 5. This is all swept away in "Chrysalis," when he is assassinated and Morgan Clark comes to power. Clark's reversal of Santiago's outward-looking policies and his role in the assassination bode ill for the station and have worrying implications for Earth and its colonies.

This comes at a time of unrest, with pro-Earth movements and Free Mars terrorists trying to force the political agenda. It is highlighted in "The War Prayer," in which the Homeguard attacks prominent aliens on the station, and in "A Voice in the Wilderness," where riots erupt on Mars. What Babylon 5 does and does very well is keep these threads alive throughout the season. Later on they will become more significant, but at this early stage they contribute to the depth of the world in which the stories operate. It is refreshing to see how much thought has gone into setting up the show and acknowledging the many facets that shape these characters' lives. In doing so it gives the series a sense of cohesion unparalleled in television science fiction and makes for a very believable world.

The same is true of the aliens on Babylon 5. The Minbari, for example, are given credibility through what the audience is told about their culture, the ruling body—the Grey Council—and how it was established by Valen, the nature of their religion, and the three castes of the Minbari and the conflicts between them. What is so clever about this is that what seems like pure background information will later become central to the story.

With the Vorlons, there is a sense that Kosh is a very "alien" character. He breathes a different atmosphere from that of Humans, he does and says things with a minimum of explanation, he is often difficult to understand, he keeps aloof from the affairs of other races, and we don't even know what he looks like. If there is one character who comes close to being totally alien, it is Kosh. His character, and that of the Vorlons, expands greatly in subsequent years, but in this first year he is very much a mystery.

Most of the aliens on Babylon 5 are Humanoid, and as in much of the genre, their cultures and their natures are extrapolated from Human life. However, they are far more rounded than most of the examples of aliens that had hitherto appeared in television science fiction. Aliens are often brought in to represent one side of Humanity, such as when a warrior race might be used in a story to examine the nature of war. While this allows science fiction to deal with subjects that mainstream drama finds difficult, Babylon 5 goes further by creating complex cultures for its main aliens and giving alien characters their own individuality within that culture. So in the case of the Narns, G'Kar is a character who has deep religious convictions, who likes the company of Earth women, and who has a vehement hatred of the Centauri and a private feud with Londo Mollari, but at the same time is prepared to make efforts to save Catherine Sakai in "Mind War." Na'Toth is more a woman of action, a Narn with no religious convictions who has contempt for G'Kar's sexual practices. While these two characters are noticeably different, they are still clearly derived from the same distinct cultural background.

In the beginning many people saw the Narn as the warrior race, while Londo of the Centauri was a figure of fun put there for some light relief. The audience was partly manipulated into making these assumptions, so viewers were surprised when other sides of the alien characters were revealed. It is now widely acknowledged to have been one of J. Michael Straczynski's masterstrokes, but it also worked against the series early on. Londo's hair was a problem for a lot of people, and it took time for many to look past that and see the richness in his character. Hair is a status symbol for the Centauri in the same way that the size of the ruffs worn by the Elizabethans indicated their status. The more hair a Centauri has sticking up, the more important he is. The problem was that in the beginning the character whom people considered to be the figure of fun was also the one with the silly hair—and it took people awhile to get over that.

When "Born to the Purple" comes along, it suddenly shows Londo as far more than a figure of fun. When he finds love with the dancing slave Adira, it allows many other sides of his character to emerge, and the audience comes to realize it has been fooled. Not only is he a man capable of love, he is also a man who has suffered loneliness. People begin to understand that behind Londo's veneer of fun is a great deal of pathos. He drinks not because he is the life and soul of the party, but because he would rather resort to alcohol than face the reality of what is happening to the Centauri Republic.

It sets him up beautifully for the arrival of Morden in "Signs and Portents." When Morden asks him, "What do you want?" it pushes all of Londo's buttons. "I want my people to reclaim their rightful place in the galaxy," he says, and, as far as Morden and his "associates" are concerned, this is the right answer. When Morden returns in "Chrysalis" and arranges for his "associates" (who, we later discover, are the Shadows) to destroy a Narn outpost, Londo turns a corner. His horror at the death of ten thousand Narns is subdued by Morden's assurances that his name is being spoken in the annals of power back on Centauri Prime. His position has changed within the galaxy. He has taken one step further down the road to darkness, and there is no turning back.

What makes the evolution of Londo's character so effective in the first year is that it was all set up right from the beginning. On the surface he seemed to be a fun-loving guy, who drinks and gambles with wild abandon. But even in the pilot, there are references to the pathos of the character when he talks about the decline of the Centauri Republic. Many people watched what was on the surface and only subconsciously registered what they were being told underneath. So Londo's move in "Signs and Portents" and later in "Chrysalis" is both prepared for and unexpected at the same time.

It is the overarching storyline that sets *Babylon 5* apart from other shows. Like a soap opera that gets people gossiping in the office the following day, it draws people into the lives of the characters and what is going to happen to them. And like a serial, it hooks people with a much larger story that has a beginning, a middle, and an end. Everything that happens contributes to the big story, and that is its appeal.

In the first year, *Babylon 5*, by telling individual stories, tries hard not to alienate its audience, so it doesn't matter if you are tuned to the arc or not. But, if you are, it is enough to hook you and make sure you tune in next time. In a series in which every piece of information could contribute to the larger picture, part of the fun is looking for those pieces of information as if they were clues to a mystery, or merely watching the story threads unravel and getting a rush of insight as a combination of things set up way down the line suddenly pays off. The first year is more about setting up than paying off, but both the way the arc works and the effect of these payoffs make themselves known in the first year. One small example is Babylon 4, how the mystery of what happened to it is set up right at the beginning of the pilot and teased again in "Grail," when Jinxo describes how it "wrinkled, twisted like putty then just disappeared." It is picked up again in "Babylon Squared," when the question of what happened to Babylon 4 is answered. We know from that moment that it traveled forward in time. But that answer is no answer because it sets up even more, bigger questions about *why* it was traveling in time.

The culmination of the first season's arc is "Chrysalis." It is clear from the episode that everything that preceded it was building to this point. Londo's association with Morden pulls the Shadows into the plot. It picks up the Narn–Centauri conflict by turning the tables on the Narn, who were seen throwing their weight around in "Midnight on the Firing Line" and are now seen to be on the receiving end. President Santiago is assassinated, pulling together all the political threads that run through the first season. Garibaldi is shot in the back, revealing his aide to have been a traitor planted right under his nose. And Delenn follows the prophecy that led her to Babylon 5 in the first place by entering the chrysalis. With one stroke, all these arc threads come to a climax that ups the stakes for the second season.

But the real hook has to be Sinclair and what happened to him at the Battle of the Line. That one line that the Minbari assassin says to him in the pilot, "There is a hole in your mind," has a resonance that continues to be felt throughout the season. Suddenly, Sinclair, who has never been able to remember the last twenty-four hours of the Earth–Minbari War, is confronted with the possibility that his missing memory could be hiding something important. Something, possibly, that could explain why the Minbari surrendered on the eve of their victory. It sets up a mystery that intrigues the audience and begins an inner battle for Sinclair as he fights his own mind to get the answers and unearth the Minbari's hidden agenda.

This whole question is teased as the season progresses, with each revelation planting enough new information to further the plot but never enough to give an answer. The Soul Hunter's words to Sinclair in the second episode, "They're using you," put Delenn in the center of the picture but don't explain why. Then, in "And the Sky Full of Stars," Sinclair is forced to relive his missing twenty-four hours by facing interrogation inside a Virtual Reality Cybernet. He finds out what happened to him on the Line, that he was taken inside the Minbari cruiser, tortured by the Grey Council, had his memory wiped, and was set free. But all this does is escalate the plot as the question changes from "What happened?" to "Why did it happen?" and adds "What was Delenn doing there?" for good measure. Then, in "Signs and Portents," Sinclair discovers that it was the Minbari who insisted he become commander of Babylon 5, again teasing the question, as Sinclair's link to the Minbari is firmly established. That is furthered in "Babylon Squared" when Delenn is summoned to the Grey Council and reiterates her reason for "playing ambassador" on Babylon 5: that she is there to study Humans because of a prophecy made by the Minbari's leading religious figure, Valen. Finally, in "Chrysalis," the answer appears to be at hand as Delenn promises to tell Sinclair about what happened at the Battle of the Line, but it is a promise that dissolves because he doesn't go to see her about it until she has entered the chrysalis. The whole season is building to this point, and the audience shares Sinclair's frustration when the answer he has spent so long searching for is taken away from him.

However, the first season of *Babylon 5* is a tremendous achievement in terms of science fiction and drama. It paints the large canvas on which the story unfolds with a richness of colors and places the characters into position while telling some good stories. All this leads very nicely into the second season, when there are bigger and better things to come.

Signs and Portents

Episode Guide

Pilot: "The Gathering"

Cast

Commander Jeffrey Sinclair	Michael O'Hare
Lt. Commander Takashima	Tamlyn Tomita
Security Chief Michael Garibaldi	Jerry Doyle
Ambassador Delenn	Mira Furlan
Ambassador G'Kar	Andreas Katsulas
Ambassador Londo Mollari	Peter Jurasik
Dr. Benjamin Kyle	Johnny Sekka
Lyta Alexander	Patricia Tallman

Guest Stars

Carolyn Sykes	Blaire Baron
Del Varner	John Fleck
The Senator	Paul Hampton
Eric	Steven A. Barnett
Kosh	Ardwright Chamberlain
Traveler	William Hayes
Tech No. 2	Linda Hoffman
Tech. No. 3	Robert Jackson
Businessman No. 1	F. William Parker
Hostage	Marianne Robertson
Businessman No. 2	David Sage
Guerra	Ed Wasser

Lyta Alexander, the first telepath sent from Earth to Babylon 5, arrives on the station as preparations are being made to greet a much more mysterious figure: a Vorlon. "No Human's even seen one," Security Chief Garibaldi tells Commander Sinclair. "Three expeditions have been sent into Vorlon space to establish formal relations. None of them came back."

Ambassador Kosh will be Babylon 5's fourth alien ambassador, joining Delenn of the Minbari, G'Kar of the Narn, and Londo Mollari of the Centauri. Sinclair, Garibaldi, and Lieutenant Commander Takashima are waiting to meet him by Docking Bay 9 when the security alarm goes off. They rush into the docking bay and, through the mist, see the Vorlon ambassador lying on the floor.

The only way Dr. Ben Kyle can hope to save Kosh is by getting inside his encounter suit, but Takashima stops him with orders from the Vorlon High Command. "They insist that the ambassador's encounter suit cannot be removed . . . for security reasons."

Sinclair knows the Vorlons don't want anyone to see what they look like, but he isn't prepared to let Kosh die. He orders all recording devices in the medlab to be turned off and relies on Kyle to adhere to his doctor's vow of confidentiality. Kyle opens the suit, and a shaft of light streams out from the crack. Kyle stares into the bright white glow with astonishment, seeing, for the first time, the face of a Vorlon.

Kyle's tests show Kosh was poisoned, but the doctor cannot save the ambassador unless he knows exactly what happened. The only way to find out is by telepathic scan, and that means Lyta Alexander.

"No! Absolutely not!" she insists at first. But Kyle eventually persuades her that lives are at stake and she enters the isolab where Kosh lies. She takes off her right glove and plunges her hand into the Vorlon's encounter suit. Her eyes snap wide open as she makes contact and flashes back to Kosh's memory of the docking bay. There is a man coming toward him with an outstretched hand. The two of them shake hands, and the man presses a poison tab onto Kosh's wrist. The contact is broken, and Lyta screams, pulling her hand away and staggering out of the isolab to identify the assassin—Commander Sinclair.

G'Kar demands that Sinclair be sent to the Vorlon homeworld for trial and conspires to ensure the Babylon 5 council votes in favor of his proposal. Meanwhile, Garibaldi has found evidence that someone smuggled on board a Changeling Net, which could make the wearer look like anyone, even Commander Sinclair.

*Sinclair and Garibaldi find the real assassin by
tracing the Changeling Net's energy source. They go in
with PPG rifles poised, but a laser blast knocks
Garibaldi to the floor almost immediately, and Sinclair
realizes he must go on alone. He stalks the corridor
until someone jumps him and knocks the PPG rifle out
of his hand. The two of them slug it out in a fist fight,
as Sinclair's opponent morphs from one person into
another. Sinclair throws him against a power grid,
and his body is bombarded with electricity until his
true form is revealed—a Minbari. The alien smiles
up at Sinclair and tells him, "There is a hole in your
mind."*

*It makes Sinclair wonder about the twenty-four-hour
period in his life he can't remember. He was at the Battle
of the Line at the end of the Earth–Minbari War when
the Minbari surrendered on the point of victory. He
never knew why.*

B*abylon 5* was just a dream in the mind of its creator,
J. Michael Straczynski, until it was given form in the
pilot, "The Gathering."

"What a rush of creativity it was," says Peter Jurasik,
whose character Londo provided the opening narration. "It
was everyone shooting from the hip. A flash of color here
and a dash of energy over there, and we were just bolting
from set to set. The characters were just emerging from the
ground in front of your eyes. They'd never been done before,
especially with an alien—you're making them up out of
whole cloth."

"There was no time to get to know the character," agrees
Andreas Katsulas, who plays G'Kar. "It was like a pre-
arranged marriage. You've had no courtship, your parents
have arranged it, and there you are: you have to unite yourself with this other person, and that's how the pilot was. A
lot of the scenes that I had were in council chambers, G'Kar
at his windup, speech-making peak, trying to persuade and
argue and fight, so it demanded an energy—it's just sink or
swim. I remember the first day, and I had a series of scenes

where there was no time to say, 'Well, can't I maybe color this a little differently?' No, it was just go blind with instinct headlong into the fire."

"It was the first TV pilot I had ever shot," remembers Michael O'Hare, who took command in "The Gathering" as Sinclair. "It's a particular demand to shoot a pilot because it's designed to see if the show's going to be bought and if many more episodes are going to be shot, so it was an extraordinary amount of pressure. I spent a lot of time just lying exhausted on the floor of the lobby when I wasn't out in front of the camera."

"I think Jay Leno said it best," adds Jerry Doyle (Garibaldi). "When they asked him about his first time hosting the *Tonight* show, he said it was like sex for the first time. It didn't actually go the way you wanted it to, it was over too quick—and you couldn't wait to do it again!"

For the writer Joe Straczynski, who was finally getting a chance to see his vision come alive, it was an attempt to show off the complex world of *Babylon 5* to a new audience. "It was fairly complex, and I realized in retrospect that I tried to cram too much stuff in," he says. "I was desperate to establish the world and then get moving. The theory, you must understand, was you would have the pilot and the very next week you would have the show. It was never meant to be a stand-alone. It's like an introduction to the show. But the way it was sold, the pilot aired first, and then nine months later came the series. Had I known that was going to be the game plan, I would have written it very differently. I would have spent a little less time on backgrounding and exposition and a little bit more time on character stuff and more on action."

A lot of action scenes and character moments became the victims of the editor's scissors, and around twenty minutes of material ended up on the cutting-room floor. "I wasn't used to being an executive producer at the time. I'd never had the final cut before," explains Straczynski. "In that kind of situation you can go one of two ways: you can abuse it and go nuts or you can be cautious. I went the latter route.

When the director turned over his cut, even though a lot of things bothered me about it, I was not confident enough of my skills as an editor or anything to say 'Okay, I'm going to redo this now.' It still bothers me that I hadn't stood up for what I thought we should be doing."

Some scenes disappeared entirely while others were shortened. Small character moments were often lost, like Laurel Takashima's admission to using the hydroponics garden to grow real coffee, a habit later transferred to Ivanova in the series, and Sinclair persuading a Human not to have sex with an exotic alien because her species eat their mates afterward. The most significant casualties, however, were the subplots involving Delenn and Sinclair's love interest, Carolyn Sykes.

One of the strongest scenes in "The Gathering," for example, where Sinclair tells Carolyn about his experiences at the Battle of the Line, was originally twice the length. "It was my favorite scene of the film," says Michael O'Hare. "From the actor's viewpoint, character is the most important thing, and it's the first thing to go. The scene you see in the pilot is a very much tourniqueted version of the scene that was actually shot. One of the problems in shooting a pilot is that you have more shot than you use, and, unfortunately, scenes that have to do with character, in other words with a more personal view toward the individuals—who's the woman in his life? what's her view of things?—are the sorts of things you get more in the series."

Carolyn was originally supposed to meet with Delenn and be decisive in persuading her to help the commander. Delenn initially refuses, explaining she is only on Babylon 5 as an observer, but later decides "It is not enough simply to observe." The final confrontation with the Changeling Net alien originally had a section where Sinclair and Garibaldi are trapped in the alien sector, unable to breathe its poisonous air, until Delenn, using surprising strength and speed, rescues both of them.

In fact, much about Delenn in the pilot is different from what she became in the series. She was supposed to be an androgynous alien played by an actress but with a masculine voice. "It would really help to sell the alien," was Joe Straczynski's original thought. "You have a male character with very female mannerisms and a very androgynous look. Then the *male* Delenn would have gone into the chrysalis [at the end of the first season] and not only emerged partly Human but female as well. But the effect on the voice with the technology that we had then was not terrific. It really didn't sound proper. My feeling was if we couldn't make it work we weren't going to do it, so I went back to her original voice."

For Mira Furlan, who plays Delenn, the experience was not a pleasant one. "I remember my pain and frustration and unhappiness at being covered with all the makeup. I thought, 'This is the end.' They wanted to change my voice, and they wanted to put lenses into my eyes. That really brought me to the stage where I was saying, 'Is this what they need me for? Neither my face is good enough nor my voice? Not even my eyes?'."

Mira had recently escaped civil war in the former Yugoslavia and left behind a successful career in films and on the stage. When she first joined *Babylon 5*, she was still trying to adjust to life in the United States. "It kind of was in some strange accord with my life at that time," she reflects. "My whole world was disrupted and in that way my whole persona, my private persona with the language, with the context, the country—everything that I knew was completely destroyed, and so was my acting personality. I was not who I was before. I had to, as they say, 'reinvent myself.' But on the other hand, I was very happy to find my work again and to find my profession again . . . I definitely learned a lot through it, but it was painful."

Despite some reservations, the pilot was successful on many levels. First and foremost, it was strong enough to ensure that a series followed, but moreover it established the background, the environment, and the look of *Babylon 5*. It also set up the central mystery of Kosh and what lay inside his encounter suit. At that stage, it was a secret Joe Straczynski was keeping almost entirely to himself. "That was pretty amazing," says Patricia Tallman, who had to scan Kosh as Babylon 5's first telepath Lyta Alexander. "Joe told me something that no one would know for the next four years about the Vorlons. He told me, 'You're seeing God, you're touched by God, you're becoming a disciple.' And I never told anyone."

1
"Midnight on the Firing Line"

Cast

Commander Jeffrey Sinclair ....Michael O'Hare
Lt. Commander Susan Ivanova ....Claudia Christian
Security Chief Michael Garibaldi ....Jerry Doyle
Ambassador Delenn ....Mira Furlan
Dr. Stephen Franklin ....Richard Biggs
Talia Winters ....Andrea Thompson
Vir Cotto ....Stephen Furst
Lennier ....Bill Mumy
Na'Toth ....Caitlin Brown
Ambassador G'Kar ....Andreas Katsulas
Ambassador Londo Mollari ....Peter Jurasik

Guest Stars

The Senator ....Paul Hampton
Carn Mollari ....Peter Trencher
Centauri No. 1 ....Jeff Austin
Kosh ....Ardwright Chamberlain
Newsperson ....Maggie Egan
Narn Captain ....Mark Hendrickson
Delta 7 ....Douglas E. McCoy
Tech. No. 1 ....Marianne Robertson

A flash of light and a jump point opens, spilling a fleet of ships out into the space around the agricultural colony Ragesh 3. "Notify Centauri Prime! Tell them we're under attack!" cries a Centauri as the ships open fire and blast him into oblivion.

On Babylon 5, Centauri ambassador Londo Mollari discovers that the attack was the work of his people's old enemy, the Narn. He is enraged at the slaughter of unarmed civilians and worried about his nephew, Carn

Mollari. It was Londo who arranged for him to work on Ragesh 3 because he thought it would be safe. "If Carn is dead, then there will be war," he tells Sinclair. "Today, tomorrow, the day after, it doesn't matter . . . There will be war."

It adds to the problems of the Human command staff on Babylon 5. Earth is caught up in the election of a new president, while raiders are hitting supply ships with weapons more powerful than standard raider guns. A newly assigned telepath, Talia Winters, has arrived and is finding it difficult to introduce herself to Lieutenant Commander Ivanova. "You will excuse me," Ivanova says, avoiding Talia's gaze, "but I'm in the middle of fifteen things, all of them annoying."

Londo has drunk himself into a crazed state. He has heard what his government intends to do about the attack on Ragesh 3. "The great Centauri Republic, the lion of the galaxy, will do nothing!" he screams at Vir, hurling a bottle of booze against the wall and shattering it into tiny pieces. He asks the other worlds at the council meeting to intervene. But Narn ambassador G'Kar informs the council that the Centauri have refused to go to the aid of their own outpost and shows a message from Londo's nephew explaining that Ragesh 3 invited the Narns to their world.

Londo, seeing he will get no help from the Babylon 5 council, decides to take matters into his own hands. But on his way down the corridor, he collides with Talia Winters, and his thoughts of killing G'Kar are so strong, they flash into her mind. Moments later, Garibaldi confronts Londo and threatens to kill him if he dares attack the Narn ambassador. Londo knows he is beaten for the moment, but he has seen his death in a dream and believes one day he will die with his hands around G'Kar's neck. "It seems I am still on target for my appointment twenty years from now," he says.

Sinclair returns from a mission to confront the

raiders, bringing with him a Narn hostage and evidence that the attack on Ragesh 3 was unprovoked. It is enough to bargain with G'Kar to get his forces to withdraw.

Ivanova sits at the bar as news filters in of Luis Santiago's impending victory in the Earth presidential election. Talia Winters joins her, and Ivanova explains that her mother was a telepath. She was forced to take drugs to suppress her talent when she refused to join the Psi Corps or go to prison. "The light in her eyes just went out bit by bit," she says, "and when we thought she could go no further, she took her own life." Talia is sorry about what happened to her mother but explains that the law is designed to stop telepaths from invading others' privacy. She hopes their relationship can start over again on better terms. "I very much doubt it," says Ivanova, and turns away.

"I wanted to open up the show more than I did before," says Joe Straczynski, "take it out in space, show the starfuries, which were not known in the pilot—there wasn't time and we weren't ready—and to compensate by having a little more in the way of character stuff and action. A lot of folks responded well to those changes."

One of those folks was Peter Jurasik, who saw his character of Londo expand in some emotional directions not seen in the pilot. "What was great about it was that it did start to access some of the heavier tones in the character—which was wonderful to play," he says. "The comedic stuff was always at hand, or on face, for Londo—that was the delight. It was the hook of the character; you kind of wanted to go to a party with him. But what was wonderful about this was that Joe, really early on, was laying down the seeds for some heavier tones."

The Narn invasion of Ragesh 3 placed G'Kar and Londo at each other's throats for the first time. "Nothing like getting your hands around an old Narn neck!" says Peter. "There was a certain desperation in that. Joe likes to have hand-to-hand combat, and I really delight in any script where I can get my hands around a Narn neck."

"The Ragesh 3 thing began to set up the whole Narn-Centauri conflict, which would play off pretty much through the course of the series," says Joe. "I wanted to get that thread in motion. I wanted to show that this is not just about the station: this place is a nexus for a lot of different locations to come together, that this is a big-canvas story. The very first episode also sets up the political election back home, and we would play into that through the rest of that season, culminating in the last episode with the assassination of President Santiago."

The first episode also brought with it quite a few changes. Laurel Takashima disappeared, as did Dr. Ben Kyle and Lyta Alexander. Delenn's appearance, and to some extent her character, was also altered. After Joe had decided that a woman playing an androgynous alien with a male voice wasn't going to work, Delenn became more feminine and her makeup was softened, much to the relief of the actress. "I had so much more freedom," says Mira Furlan. "It was a whole different experience, and I enjoyed it very much. I enjoyed having my mouth, my nose, my cheeks, my neck. It was still a lot to deal with, but it brought me back to myself somehow."

The changes had a substantial impact on the storyline, particularly in the loss of certain characters' story arcs when the characters themselves disappeared. But there was never any thought of starting afresh and pretending the pilot never happened. "My feeling is fiction, like life, is open to changes, and let's use that to our benefit," says Joe Straczynski. "I just felt that we could use it as ammunition. So we referred to all the characters who weren't there anymore at various points in the story, and I made a few changes here and there. Originally, Takashima was going to be the one who shot Garibaldi in the back [in "Chrysalis"] or was involved in that conspiracy. That was a loss, but I just figured, 'Let's use it.' "

"Midnight on the Firing Line" was always intended to be

the first show broadcast, but it was actually filmed fourth. Unlike those in later seasons, many of the first-season episodes were filmed out of order to allow for getting the special effects finished in time or, in the case of "Midnight," getting the sets built.

However, for Andrea Thompson, who joined *Babylon 5* as the station's new telepath, it really was her first time on the show. "I remember walking onto the set, the main corridor, and I just got chills in my spine," she says. "I was always a science fiction fan since I was a kid. I grew up on it and really loved it. It was just a really magical experience, and I felt that I was part of something really important, something really big."

She admits to being a little nervous in her first scene, introducing herself to Ivanova (Claudia Christian) in the Observation Dome. "It was the first day of filming, and I wanted to do really well, and it was a little bit intimidating. Even actors get starstruck sometimes, and it was the idea of working on this science fiction series that I was starstruck over. So they rolled the first take, and I walk out, and I say, 'I'm Talia Winters, licensed commercial *psychopath!*' Claudia just roared and broke into laughter. The whole crew did, and I had to join them because it was really kind of funny. That really broke the ice, and we went on to shoot the scene. I went on to be very close with Claudia. We spent many afternoons drinking champagne after that."

It was also the first episode that Andrea got to meet and work with Jerry Doyle, who later became her husband in real life. Their first scene was in the transport tube, where she asks Garibaldi for his advice about approaching Ivanova. "We rehearsed it several times, and it went very smoothly. Then we rolled, and I go up, press the elevator button, and the doors open and there's Jerry standing there with his arms crossed and his trousers down around his ankles! It was really a pretty priceless moment. There were a lot of laughs that day.

"But it made the scene easier to shoot," she continues. "Oftentimes, especially when you know the cameras are rolling, you get a little tense and a little uptight, and I've always found it's the best way to make a scene work if you're not really focusing. I know a lot of people who are method actors, and they have to be really concentrated and all that, but for me it always works best if I'm laughing and loose beforehand."

Talia's introduction culminates in the scene toward the end where she finally gets to talk to Ivanova in the casino bar. It helps explain a little more about telepaths, the Psi Corps, and the laws that apply to people with psychic ability. It also brings into focus the friction between the two characters as Ivanova explains how her mother suffered at the hands of the Psi Corps, the organization that Talia represents.

"It was the first time that you saw any quality other than being uptight and very militaristic," says Claudia Christian (Ivanova). "I think it was good in showing her very tough façade slowly etched away by this person who has such insistence in talking to her. It was one of the nicer moments in *Babylon* 5, one of the most tender. And it was heavily laced with sexual overtones when we were shooting it because Andrea and I were just joking around so much."

This scene was followed (after the commercial break) by Garibaldi showing Delenn his second favorite thing in the universe. This turns out to be the classic cartoon *Duck Dodgers in the 24½th Century*, which had the added bonus of being owned by Warner Bros., avoiding any royalty payments to show the clip.

"[It showed] A whole new element in Delenn's character, which doesn't come often," says Mira Furlan. "There are a couple of scenes like that throughout the whole series—you can count them on the fingers of one hand, the so-called funny scenes. I enjoyed it very much, and I would love to do more of that stuff."

"I thought Mira was good in that," says Jerry Doyle. "I remember we were sitting there looking at a blank screen—they weren't showing us the cartoon; they laid that in later—and as we were doing the popcorn thing, I remember her picking up a kernel of popcorn and looking at it. Another actor might have picked up some popcorn and started eating, but she [Delenn] had never seen popcorn before, so she was intrigued by what this food item was. Then I laughed because of what she did. What she did made it real for me in that moment, and when I was laughing, it was more at her and her spin on the scene than at the cartoon."

2
"Soul Hunter"

Cast
Commander Jeffrey Sinclair ....Michael O'Hare
Lt. Commander Susan Ivanova ....Claudia Christian
Security Chief Michael Garibaldi ....Jerry Doyle
Ambassador Delenn ....Mira Furlan
Dr. Stephen Franklin ....Richard Biggs
Talia Winters ....Andrea Thompson
Vir Cotto ....Stephen Furst
Lennier ....Bill Mumy
Na'Toth ....Caitlin Brown
Ambassador G'Kar ....Andreas Katsulas
Ambassador Londo Mollari ....Peter Jurasik

Guest Stars
The Soul Hunter ....W. Morgan Sheppard
Soul Hunter No. 2 ....John Snyder
Med. Tech. No. 1 ....Toni Attell
Man ,...Jim Bentley
Tech. No. 1 ....Mark Conley
Guard No. 1 ....David D. Darling
Guard No. 2 ....Ted W. Henning
Tech. No. 2 ....Marianne Robertson

An alien of an unknown species lies unconscious in the isolab. Delenn thinks she may be able to identify him, but as soon as she catches a glimpse of his face, she grabs Garibaldi's gun from his holster and aims it through the glass. "Kill it!" she cries. "It is a Soul Hunter."

When the Soul Hunter awakes, he watches closely as Dr. Franklin battles to save the life of a man who was stabbed in Down-Below. "Dull, muffled, slower now," whispers the Hunter as the man's body goes into shock. "A shadow. The long exhalation of the spirit," he says as the man's life slips away in front of him. The doctors

shock the patient, trying to stimulate life, but it is no
good and he dies on the table. The Hunter sighs and
closes his eyes, as if he felt the man's passing.

Soul Hunters are drawn to death, where they claim to
collect the souls of the dying to preserve them. But the
Minbari believe souls do not die: they are reborn into the
next generation. "Remove those souls and the whole
suffers," Delenn tells the Soul Hunter. She vows to find
his collection and release it.

A second Soul Hunter arrives at Babylon 5,
demanding to see Sinclair. He tells him his "brother" is
disturbed after failing many soul-collecting missions. He
is no longer satisfied to wait for the moment of death;
instead he kills to add to his collection. "Someone is
about to die, Commander," says the second Soul Hunter.
"And it will be at his hands." Sinclair's first thought is of
Delenn.

The Soul Hunter has captured Delenn and secured her
to a table where tubes trail from her arteries, ready to
take away her lifeblood. Above her is a machine and an
empty sphere to capture her soul. The machine powers
up and begins to draw the life force from her body. The
Soul Hunter catches a glimpse and gasps. "You plan
such a thing? Incredible."

Using the second Soul Hunter to sense Delenn's
impending death, Sinclair stalks close to where she is
being held. He is leapt on by the Soul Hunter who
throws him up against the wall and bellows in his face.
"Don't you understand? She is Satai . . . They're using
you." The Soul Hunter throws Sinclair to the ground,
and he turns to see the life being sucked out of Delenn's
body. Instinctively, Sinclair spins the machine around
until its power is centered on the Soul Hunter. It pulls at
the Hunter's soul until every drop of life is drained from
him. The sphere inside the machine fills with a warm
glow as his lifeless body collapses.

Delenn recovers in medlab, regaining consciousness
briefly as Sinclair and Franklin stand over her. "I knew
you would come," she says, smiling up at Sinclair. "We

*were right about you." Later, in his quarters, Sinclair
looks up the reference to Satai. He finds it is an honorific
title applied to the Minbari ruling body, the Grey
Council. "Why would a member of their ruling body be
assigned to ambassadorial duties?" he asks.*

*The Soul Hunters are banished from the station,
leaving behind only a collection of soul spheres. Delenn
sits with them softly glowing in a bag by her side. She
takes one lovingly and crushes it with her fingers. She
sighs as she feels something brush past her face and drift
away to freedom.*

For most people, "Soul Hunter" was where *Babylon 5*
started to live up to expectations. All the elements are
there: a good story, strong characterization, action, pace, special effects, and a contribution to the story arc. But, as
writer and executive producer Joe Straczynski recalls, things
might not have been that way. "There was a previous draft of
that script, which was vastly different from the one that got
produced. I think the first one I actually wrote was 'Soul
Hunter'—first or second—that was the one that was closest
to my head. After I finished it and it got distributed, I looked
at it again and said, 'This is crap,' and I recalled all the
copies and sent out a memo to say I was momentarily pos-
sessed by an idiot!"

The rewritten version sets up a debate about the nature
of life, whether sentient beings really have souls. Delenn and
the Soul Hunter clearly believe they do, but Franklin believes
it is all patent superstition and Sinclair doesn't know what to
believe. "If they are actually there is anyone's guess," says
Joe. "I carefully don't address that issue in the course of the
script. My job is not to provide people with answers. My job
as a storyteller is to ask questions and provoke discussions
and start bar fights. People tell me, 'Well, you didn't say if
souls are real or not.' Well, yeah, that's right. What do you
think? I wanted people to look at what they think about stuff
and go from there rather than my just giving them all the
answers. That was also one of the very first ones to divide
the fans strongly between those who want their science very

literal—they don't want any kind of metaphysics at all—and those who welcome that sort of thing."

The question of souls is central to the story arc, feeding into Sinclair's missing twenty-four hours at the Battle of the Line and the Minbari's reasons for insisting he be assigned to Babylon 5. In many ways, the discussion about the nature of souls prepares for the moment in Season Two's "Points of Departure" when Lennier reveals Sinclair has a Minbari soul. This is something Delenn already knows and is the reason why she is on Babylon 5 "playing ambassador." When she tells him, "I knew you would come," she is sensing Valen, and when the Soul Hunter says, "They're using you," he is referring to the Minbari's manipulation of Sinclair into a position from which he can become their great religious leader.

None of this is apparent at this stage. The truth about Sinclair won't even be known until the latter half of the third season, but it is all being set up for later. This episode also fills in some necessary background regarding the death of the former Minbari leader Dukhat and how the Earth–Minbari War started. Like many of the episodes in the first season, it is laying in plot threads that don't show their significance until later on. "Soul Hunter" does this successfully by setting up an anticipation of what is to come without detracting from the main story.

Another bonus for the story was W. Morgan Sheppard, whose portrayal of the Soul Hunter impressed many people. "I enjoyed working with him immensely," says Mira Furlan, who plays Delenn. "I think he's terrific. He has such a theater background, which reminded me of my past in Yugoslavia, all the stories, the theater stories, the old actors. It was as if I were thrown back into the theater, the heavy stage acting with which I was so familiar. The European flair was there, and we had a nice time working together."

Morgan Sheppard worked hard with the director, Jim Johnston, to create an alienness for his character. "It was Morgan's idea about walking," says Jim. "He said, 'I don't want it to appear that I'm walking: I want it to appear that I'm floating.' So we designed this long gown that he wore so that we wouldn't see his feet move, and he created this little walk

where you couldn't see his legs moving. He did seem to sort
of float, as if he was on a skateboard being pulled down the
corridor, and I thought it was a great turn. He brought a lot to
the part, and it's certainly one of my favorite episodes."

"Soul Hunter" was the first episode for Jim Johnston, who
became one of *Babylon 5*'s most prolific directors. He directed six episodes in the first year alone. His background is
in commercials, where he learned about special effects, and
he joined *Babylon 5* after five years of working on action
shows like *Miami Vice*, *The Equalizer*, and *Tour of Duty*. This
was his first experience of science fiction. "I immediately took
to it," he says. "One of the things I liked about *Babylon 5*
was the sets that they had. They had sets that allowed me
to move the camera, so I could use steadicam. They had
long corridors, and I could do endless dolly moves. And they
weren't afraid of the dark. Many television shows are afraid
to let it go to the dark side as far as cinematography goes,
and they weren't. 'Soul Hunter' I thought was kind of mysterious and dark anyway, so I wanted to keep it that way, and
they allowed me to do that."

Perhaps the most effective scene in "Soul Hunter," in
visual terms, is at the end, when Delenn crushes the glass
spheres, releasing the souls into the atmosphere, where
they dance past the wind chimes in her room. This relied
a great deal on the special effects added in postproduction
by Ron Thornton and his team at Foundation Imaging. "I
thought it was visually very nice crushing those spheres,"
says Jim Johnston. "I had them bring in little chimes [for the
set]. I thought that would be a nice touch to show that souls
were departing, so I could cut in little tinkly chime sounds
which I thought would make a moving scene. I'm glad I
added the sound effect, because when you were shooting it
you didn't know how beautiful it would be because you had
to rely on Ron to put that in at the end."

"You have to imagine a lot of things on *Babylon*," says
Mira. "You have your own vision which is completely different to what you see on the screen. So sometimes it's
really weird. I kind of communicated with those little balls,
loved them very much."

The episode was a very strong one for Delenn because it explored her character in far greater depth than had been possible in previous episodes. Here, we see her gentleness with the soul spheres, her strength when she tries to kill the Soul Hunter, and the mystery surrounding her plans on Babylon 5. "What's so great in this role is I can combine the toughness and the gentleness," says Mira. "Usually it's either one or the other. It's rare that all those character traits are put together in a character . . . Sometimes when I watch it ['Soul Hunter'] today, I think I made a lot of mistakes. I would have done it differently. That's why I don't like to watch myself. I'm not one of those actors—I don't have the ability to detach myself from the acting."

The episode also introduces Dr. Franklin, with a quick explanation of what happened to his predecessor, Dr. Kyle, who appeared in the pilot. It was the second episode for actor Richard Biggs, who had already filmed the fourth episode, "Infection." Filming out of order is often difficult in terms of character development, but in this case, it actually helped the actor establish himself as Dr. Franklin. "By the second episode I had caught my breath, and I was paddling around," he says. "I had gotten a little bit more secure and a little bit more relaxed and then got to play the entrance of the character."

The success of the episode meant that "Soul Hunter" became an early benchmark for the season. It worked on many levels, in terms of story, themes, and its contribution to the arc. "I love that it blended the scientific with the mystical," concludes Joe Straczynski. "I love the Soul Hunter concept. I love the way Morgan Sheppard did the role. And it helped me to tell a story where the characters really got involved. It was a good story for Delenn, certainly. I'm very partial to that one."

3
"Born to the Purple"

Cast

Commander Jeffrey Sinclair ....Michael O'Hare
Lt. Commander Susan Ivanova ....Claudia Christian
Security Chief Michael Garibaldi ....Jerry Doyle
Ambassador Delenn ....Mira Furlan
Dr. Stephen Franklin ....Richard Biggs
Talia Winters ....Andrea Thompson
Vir Cotto ....Stephen Furst
Lennier ....Bill Mumy
Na'Toth ....Caitlin Brown
Ambassador G'Kar ....Andreas Katsulas
Ambassador Londo Mollari ....Peter Jurasik

Guest Stars

Adira Tyree ....Fabiana Udenio
Trakis ....Clive Revill
Ko'Dath ....Mary Woronov
Ock ....Jimm Giannini
Andrei Ivanova ....Robert Phalen
Norg ....Robert DiTillio
Gunman No. 1 ....Tom Lowe
Dancer ....Katharine Mills
Butz ....Mike Norris
Gera Akshi ....Laura Peterson
Tech. No. 1 ....Marianne Robertson
Dr. Goyokin ....Momo Yashima

Londo is enchanted by the young, beautiful Centauri dancer on the stage in front of him. "Is she not perfection?" he says as Adira Tyree moves her slender Centauri body to the music. Later, back in his quarters, he finds her waiting for him in bed.

Londo is supposed to be negotiating with G'Kar over the Euphrates Treaty, except that he is too wrapped up in his newfound love to care. But he doesn't know that

Adira is working for someone else. Trakis wants her to steal Londo's Purple Files, a secret collection of slander that has kept Londo's family in a position of power for many years. She doesn't want to do it, but as a slave she has no choice. "When you've done your job you'll have your freedom," Trakis tells her, "and I'll have the Centauri Republic by its mighty neck."

Garibaldi has discovered someone is using the Gold Channel to make illicit transmissions back to Earth, and he's determined to track down the culprit. But he can trace the caller only so far before his system is hit by a wall program.

Londo slumps in his chair as the drug Adira put in his drink takes effect. She puts a mind probe to his temple, gets him to tell her the access codes to his Purple Files, and transfers them to a data crystal. She kisses him tenderly on the forehead. "I'm sorry, Londo," she says, and looks back at him one last time before walking out of the door.

Adira is supposed to hand the files over to Trakis, but she runs out on their meeting and Trakis seeks help from Londo. "Adira has betrayed us both," he says and plants a listening device on Londo's back.

Londo knows his career is over if his government finds out his Purple Files have been stolen and asks Sinclair for his assistance and his discretion. Sinclair agrees, if in return Londo gives him his assurance that he will compromise on the Euphrates Treaty. They discover where Adira is hiding, but Trakis is listening and he finds her first.

Sinclair goes back to his peacemaking duties, this time with G'Kar. In return for certain concessions, he tells G'Kar of a trader who has something he might want to buy and arranges for Talia Winters to sit in on the deal. "My only purpose is to verify the merchandise," Talia tells the seller, who turns out to be Trakis. "So it is imperative you do not think of anything else, such as . . . where Adira Tyree is now." Suddenly his thoughts are exposed, and Talia plucks Adira's location from his mind.

Garibaldi is still trying to track down whoever's using the Gold Channel, and this time he won't be beaten by any wall program. He watches the call go through and is astonished to find it is Ivanova calling her dying father. "I haven't been the best of fathers to you," he tells her with his last breath. "I'm sorry. And ashamed. Forgive me." Tears well up in Ivanova's eyes, but despite the emotion of the moment, she holds them in.

Londo says good-bye to Adira. He asks her to stay, but she knows the wounds are too fresh. So he gives her a Centauri brooch that has been in his family for generations. "Wear it proudly as a free woman," he tells her. "And someday come back to me . . ."

"Yippee, right?" exclaims Peter Jurasik, remembering Londo's romantic liaison in "Born to the Purple." "My first memory of that was that Jerry Doyle was so upset I had a love scene before he did," he says. "He bitched about it awful. He just moaned and shuffled around. He couldn't believe the relatively short chubby character actor with the big hair was going to get the love scene first!"

It took Londo on a different path from the comic side we'd seen in "The Gathering" and the fiery side revealed in "Midnight on the Firing Line." "I mean, to take this wild insane character and put him in heartfelt romantic situations with this beautiful Italian girl who they cast—oh, God help me!—thank God I had only one day in bed with her! It was disturbing! It was a lot harder than working with Stephen Furst [Vir], I can tell you. It was a wonderful challenge to me. I never said anything to Joe, but I was truly appreciative of that because all the promises we had about [Londo] Mollari expanding and being multifaceted were in fact coming true. I just tried to respond as best as I could."

The story came out of Joe Straczynski's initial premise that Londo would get involved with a dancer and be blackmailed. "It is in my usual perverse nature that in a show

where typically the hero gets the girl, the first character to
get laid in the show is Londo! It is not what you'd expect,
necessarily, and it began to show a different side to him, that
he is a romantic. He is someone who, on some level, believes
he's a hero."

This was the premise that Joe handed over to Lawrence G.
DiTillio to flesh out into a script. "The premise he gave me,
I threw out, but that was okay with him," says Larry candidly. "Originally it had to do with dust, which was the drug
Joe created which actually showed up around the third
season. I never understood dust per se because why would
you want to take a drug that made you nuts? You generally
take a drug because it makes you feel good. I thought it was
kind of like a sleazy thing, and I wanted the story to be on a
little higher level, so I came up with the idea of the Purple
Files, the files the Centauri keep on each other to do their
deadly work.

"When Londo started out he was kind of a buffoonish
character," he continues. "He was just a kind of funny drunk,
and Joe wanted an episode to do another side of him. I
thought he's kind of a romantic figure and kind of a tragic
figure, and it would make a good story to concentrate on the
love relationship."

However, one intimate detail of the love relationship was
cut during filming. As both Londo and Vir explain in later
episodes, Centauri males have six sexual organs. Naturally,
it would follow that Centauri women have corresponding
physiology, and this was originally intended to be shown in
"Born to the Purple." "It was in the script," says Peter
Jurasik. "We were in bed together, and she's got to run off
somewhere, and she gets up and there was supposed to be
a shot from my point of view as she walked away from me
naked from behind, where we were going to see the female
Centauri genitalia, with three little marks down each side of
her back. I think when they finally put it together, everybody
looked at it and went, 'Urgh, we're not going to film this, are
we? It looks kinda weird.' "

Londo is so head-over-heels in love with Adira that he
doesn't care who sees them together, even though a Cen-

tauri ambassador should not normally be seen associating with a lowly dancer. After he tells her he doesn't care about appearances, he takes her to the finest restaurant on Babylon 5. Even at the beginning of the episode, he is happy to share his admiration of her with Sinclair and G'Kar. This is also the scene in which G'Kar comes face-to-face with the female Narn who has arrived to be his aide—the strong-willed and short-lived Ko'Dath.

"I liked that scene," says Andreas Katsulas (G'Kar). "I played it as though she was totally not what he expected, and so he's embarrassed. He's 'Oh my God, look what I've got to put up with; how am I going to handle this incredible Narn that has come here?' I think I had him spit out his drink that he was drinking when he took a look at her. It was so much fun!"

Sinclair and Londo later return to the Dark Star dance club, when they need information on Adira's whereabouts. Both of them are undercover, and the scene provoked much discussion in production meetings. Could Sinclair, they wondered, actually walk about his own station without being recognized? "The mayor of New York, if he put on a hat and an old coat and went down to the gallery, could probably walk around without being recognized," says Larry DiTillio. "Remember, Babylon 5 has a quarter of a million people jammed into the length of it, so I don't think it was outrageous to say that Sinclair could put on some kind of disguise—it wasn't much of a disguise, of course: he just got out of uniform really—and not be recognized. Maybe I was wrong, but it seemed to work for me. And what it showed was that Sinclair played by the rules, but he wasn't afraid to bend the rules when it came to helping somebody."

The other subplot, which didn't appear to be significant until the end, was Garibaldi's search for the culprit who was making unofficial use of the Gold Channel. It turned out to be Ivanova, calling the hospital where her father was dying, although for Claudia Christian, filming it was not quite as heart-wrenching as it appeared. "The fellow who was playing my father as he was in his hospital bed had this moment which didn't end up in the episode," she says. "He was coughing so much, and the camera is around my back shooting over my shoulder so they can't see my face—and I'm laughing! The crew think I'm sobbing, but in actuality I'm cracking up. There's too much coughing! And the boom operator, who's above me, who's the only one who can see my face, he's shaking, trying not to laugh, and the boom starts going up and down. People were probably very moved, thinking, 'Oh look, she's even crying off camera.' No, I was cracking up!"

It is a key moment for her character, not only in an emotional sense, but also in the way Ivanova handles her personal life. "I think it shows a lot of quiet resolve and strength," says Claudia. "It also is an indication of how bloody important her job is. I mean, yes she's hiding her feelings by immersing herself in work, but on the other hand she's a pro. [She thinks], 'I've lost everyone in my family, and I still go to work.' "

"She did a really nice job in showing the vulnerability of her character and the dignity of her position," says Jerry Doyle, who, as Garibaldi, decided not to report her misuse of the Gold Channel. "I thought the end product was really sweet because it wasn't shot in the order that you saw it. We were on the same page when it laid itself out from beginning to end. I thought it had a nice arc. It was a nice character moment for both of us."

But it is Londo's capacity to love and his capacity to be hurt by love that makes the biggest impression in "Born to the Purple." "You know, I look back at that show, and I'm not sure how good the work is from my point of view," says Peter Jurasik honestly. "But it certainly is heartfelt. It was absolutely key in a sense that it really did, for the first time, extend the character base to see how many different points we were able to touch."

"I particularly enjoyed the love affair," adds Larry DiTillio. "It was nice to show Londo as the romantic, which he really is, and to show that his flaw is that he's always been searching for love, which, of course, comes to tragic consequences in Season Three."

4
"Infection"

Cast

Commander Jeffrey Sinclair ....Michael O'Hare
Lt. Commander Susan Ivanova ....Claudia Christian
Security Chief Michael Garibaldi ....Jerry Doyle
Ambassador Delenn ....Mira Furlan
Dr. Stephen Franklin ....Richard Biggs
Talia Winters ....Andrea Thompson
Vir Cotto ....Stephen Furst
Lennier ....Bill Mumy
Na'Toth ....Caitlin Brown
Ambassador G'Kar ....Andreas Katsulas
Ambassador Londo Mollari ....Peter Jurasik

Guest Stars

Dr. Vance Hendricks ....David McCallum
Nelson Drake ....Marshall Teague
Mary Ann Cramer ....Patricia Healy
Tech. No. 1 ....Sav Farrow
Security Guard ....Daniel Hutchison
Tech. No. 2 ....Sylva Kelegian
Guard ....Tony Rizzoli
Tech. No. 3 ....Marianne Robertson
Customs Guard ....Paul Yeuell

Mary Ann Cramer, a reporter for ISN, is pestering Garibaldi about the meeting she is supposed to be having with Commander Sinclair. "If this interview hadn't been set up weeks ago," she says indignantly, "I'd swear that Commander Sinclair didn't want to be interviewed for Interstellar News Network."

Dr. Franklin's former tutor Vance Hendricks has arrived on Babylon 5 fresh from a dig on the dead world Ikaara 7, where he found some alien artifacts he wants his "favorite student" to see. Franklin is amazed to find

*they contain veins, capillaries, and traces of DNA—
evidence of organic technology. "The one trick that
Earth hasn't yet been able to crack," says Hendricks.*

*Franklin and Hendricks are so engrossed with their
study of the artifacts that they don't notice that
Hendricks's assistant, Nelson, has been infected by the
alien organism. That night, Nelson, in a feverish state,
takes one of the alien artifacts and watches as its six
beetlelike legs flex inches from his throat. They dig their
way into his flesh and glow with green energy as the two
organisms merge.*

*Nelson is transformed into an armored killing
machine. He fires a bolt of energy from the organic
weapon that has become part of his arm and knocks
Franklin sprawling across medlab. Franklin learns the
artifacts are weapons developed by the Ikaarans to wipe
out alien invaders. They were programmed with a
researcher's brainwave patterns and told to protect their
planet by destroying anything that wasn't pure Ikaaran.
But the Ikaarans found out to their cost that no one is
"pure," and the whole race was wiped out.*

*The Nelson Machine cannot be stopped by ordinary
firepower, and Sinclair decides the only way to defeat it
is to lure it into the docking area and blow it out into
space. Despite Garibaldi's protests, Sinclair takes on the
mission alone. He leads the Nelson Machine through the
station, appealing to its programmed personality,
goading it with the truth. He tells it to look inside
Nelson's mind and see what the weapons did to Ikaara.
"Dead, a thousand years dead," moans the Nelson
Machine. Screaming in pain, anguish, and realization, it
pulls the artifact from its chest. Sparks fly as it crushes
the object in its hand. Sinclair shades his eyes with his
arm, and when he looks back, Nelson is lying on the
floor with all trace of the alien armor gone from his
naked Human body.*

*Everybody is talking about how Sinclair risked his life
to save the station, but Garibaldi isn't convinced it is
heroism. He has known a lot of soldiers, like Sinclair,*

who came out of the war changed. "I think they're looking for something worth dying for, because it's easier than finding something worth living for," he tells him. The words touch something in Sinclair, but he does not have an answer for his old friend Garibaldi. "And I think maybe I should," he says.

With the alien artifacts confiscated and taken back to Earth Central, Sinclair finally has to face the ISN reporter. She wants to know if Earth's venture into space is really worth it. Sinclair replies that one day the sun will go cold, taking with it everything Humanity has achieved. "All this was for nothing," he tells her, "unless we go to the stars."

The first episode to go in front of the cameras at the beginning of the season was "Infection," and that is what colors most people's memories of making it. "It was one of those shows," says Joe Straczynski. "We shot it first because it would be the easiest one to shoot, and we were still breaking in the sets. Literally, we had paint crews preceding us. We're shooting in stage A, and they're painting and insulating and wiring up stage B!"

While the home of Babylonian Productions was being changed from a warehouse into a studio, a new crew was getting used to working together, and new actors were getting acquainted with the characters they were going to be playing for several years to come. "Infection" was one of the biggest episodes for Richard Biggs as Dr. Franklin, but his very first day on the set was one of his worst experiences on the show. "It was terrible," he says. "I came in in the middle of the episode; I was the new kid on the block on a Friday night. It was the last scene of the day. Everyone was under a lot of pressure. I had six lines on the Observation Deck, a lot of techno mumbo jumbo, and I hit my mark, and *sixteen* takes later they finally got it. I remember Michael O'Hare coming to me after sixteen takes; he patted me on the back and said [in a sarcastic tone], 'Welcome to *Babylon 5*.' "

The show has occasionally brought in prominent guest stars as a way of attracting viewers to the series. Majel Barrett in

Season Three's "Point of No Return" was an example of that because of her links with *Star Trek*. Here, it was the well-known British actor David McCallum who came in to play Vance Hendricks. "He was a quiet man," says Richard Biggs. "I always wanted to rehearse the scene and change the scene, and he wasn't quite there working it. [Instead] he'd come to my trailer and say, 'How about this?' or 'How about that?' . . . I wanted to point out that relationship. The characters were old friends—he was a teacher of mine—and I would have liked to have investigated those relationships a little bit more."

Instead, it was Hendricks's discovery of organic technology that took center stage. It firmly establishes it as part of the *Babylon 5* universe and introduces Earth's desire to develop organic technology for itself. For the Ikaarans, however, it had disastrous consequences, and their misguided notion of purity is very much the message of the episode. "At the time we were hearing a lot about 'racial cleansing' going on, and it bugs me when somebody says that racial purity must be maintained," says Joe Straczynski. "No single race is one hundred percent pure of anything. There is a certain logic when he [Sinclair] says, 'When you become obsessed with the enemy, you *become* the enemy.' In this country, during the fifties, we had the McCarthy hearings in which they were terrified over the communists controlling the state. And in pursuing their reaction to that, they became the controlling interests of the state. It became that which they feared or were fighting against. There's a certain logic there that people have to be reminded about once in a while. It's my obligation as a writer not just to entertain, but every once in so often to kick the viewer in the side and say, 'Look, pay attention, don't do this.' "

It didn't quite turn out the way he would have liked, however. *Babylon 5* is innovative in many respects, but the concept of a man in a rubber suit is a little too reminiscent of the monster-of-the-week science fiction shows that had typified much of the genre up to this point. "I should have learned my lesson about rubber-suit monsters, and I hadn't," he says candidly. "This wasn't as well presented as it might have been. And again, as the first episode was edited I did okay on it, better than the pilot, but I was still learning."

The episode doesn't quite do justice to the idea lying at its heart. Sinclair's confrontation with the Nelson Machine spells out the moral of the story and is, perhaps, a little heavy-handed. "I tell you there was a lot of good writing in that, but the trouble is it doesn't really play as well as it might," says Michael O'Hare (Sinclair). "On the page, the writing is good, but in reality, with my experiences with physical danger, when you're involved chasing a madman who's trying to kill everybody, you don't have long epistemological discussions with him where you hold forth and philosophically try to ponder the error of his way. You just try to catch him."

Where the episode succeeds is in showing Sinclair's foolhardy heroics in fighting the Nelson Machine single-handedly, something Garibaldi forces him to face. It was "the scene that everyone was startled by," according to Joe Straczynski. "Normally you don't ask the hero that question: why do you do it? He didn't have a good answer. He was someone casting about for a reason to live, and eventually he would find that; it would take him a thousand years of time travel to do it [in Season Three's 'War Without End'], but he would eventually find that."

"Straczynski wrote that scene in order to make for an interesting argument of perspective to stop the leader rolling up his sleeves and getting in there himself and risking his life," says Michael O'Hare. "At that time in my life, I was going through some particular things that were not related to the show at all, other parts of my life, in which I was very much looking for something to believe in. So much that I did believe in had disappointed me, so I identified with someone who's looking for something with some honor to it and was willing to risk his life over that."

It is the strength of the relationship between Sinclair and Garibaldi that makes a scene like that possible. Garibaldi mentions here how he and Sinclair met on Mars and how it was Sinclair's friendship that led to his getting the job on Babylon 5, and it is this solid friendship that repeatedly gives the audience access to the characters' thoughts and feelings. "What makes the show appealing—or any show appealing for that matter—is when you learn the intricacies of the characters, their likes and dislikes and their fears and their passions," says Jerry Doyle, who plays Garibaldi. "When you come to know them as individuals rather than characters, then you can sympathize and empathize and care. Our show was originally put into this area of 'science fiction,' which, for some reason, wasn't really dealt with as 'real TV' or 'regular TV' . . . I always felt that the show was a one-hour drama that happened to be in the science fiction genre. You have to survive based on the fact it is a drama that holds your attention, that you do care about the characters, that you do rise and fall with them, that you laugh and cry with them."

The episode ends by concentrating on the larger character of space itself, as Sinclair explains to ISN why Humanity should stay in space. The speech has resonances of President Kennedy, who launched America into the space race in 1961 by announcing that a man would set foot on the moon by the end of the decade. "When I was a boy he was talking about space exploration on television," says Michael. "I tried to keep him in mind and how much he meant to me when I was a young man. But the practical realities of giving that speech? There was nothing but noise through the whole damn thing! It hardly allowed me any concentration; it drove me crazy. The set was so noisy in those days. I'm very fond of complete silence when I work. It's just me. I'm very fond of the crew, but it was noisy at the beginning."

The episode was originally going to include newsreel footage of an earlier speech by Kennedy, calling on people to be pioneers moving toward a New Frontier, although this was subsequently dropped. Sinclair's speech stands up well enough on its own and was "an important thing to do," according to Joe Straczynski, and one of the best things about "Infection," from his point of view. "Some parts of it I like," he says, "and parts of it I wouldn't mind if they all vanished off a pier somewhere."

5
"The Parliament of Dreams"

Cast

Commander Jeffrey Sinclair ....Michael O'Hare
Lt. Commander Susan Ivanova ....Claudia Christian
Security Chief Michael Garibaldi ....Jerry Doyle
Ambassador Delenn ....Mira Furlan
Dr. Stephen Franklin ....Richard Biggs
Talia Winters ....Andrea Thompson
Vir Cotto ....Stephen Furst
Lennier ....Bill Mumy
Na'Toth ....Caitlin Brown
Ambassador G'Kar ....Andreas Katsulas
Ambassador Londo Mollari ....Peter Jurasik

Guest Stars

Catherine Sakai ....Julia Nickson
Tu'Pari ....Thomas Kopache
Narn No. 1 ....Joy Hardin
Du'Rog ....Mark Hendrickson
Guard ....Calvin Jung
Businessman No. 1 ....Randall Kirby
Pilgrim ....Michael McKenzie
Dome Tech ....Marianne Robertson
Head Waiter ....Glenn Robinson
Businessman No. 2 ....Erich Martin Von Hicks

*G'Kar's dinner is interrupted by the arrival of
Diplomatic Courier Tu'Pari with a message from his old
adversary Du'Rog, who tells him he will soon be dead.
"Already my agent is close to you," he says. G'Kar
ponders his words as his new attaché, Na'Toth, walks
through the door.*

It is a week of exchanging religious ideas on Babylon 5,

and the command staff and alien ambassadors are attending a magnificent Centauri banquet. Londo—drunk to the point of hysteria—is laughing wildly, but Sinclair isn't caught up in the atmosphere like the others. As he slinks away from the party, Londo scrambles onto the table, pushes food and statues out of his way, and passes out in front of everyone.

Sinclair watches Catherine Sakai. She catches his eye, and they stand facing each other, awkwardly. She apologizes for being there when she promised to stay away from him, but instead of being angry, he invites her to dinner. It is something they repeat about every two or three years. "The dance goes something like this," says Catherine. "You ask about my aunt, I ask about your brother, we lie about not missing each other, then we end up in bed together." Moments later he is asking about her aunt and she about his brother, and they laugh.

Delenn has been sent a new aide from Minbar, Lennier of the Third Fane of Chu'Domo, who helps her with the Minbari rebirth ceremony. Delenn, dressed in white robes, recites the words of Valen as small red fruits are passed around the assembled guests. "This is your death," she says. "Taste of it and be not afraid." Delenn looks Sinclair in the eyes and then swallows the fruit.

That night Catherine arrives at Sinclair's quarters but soon regrets her decision and is about to go, when Sinclair takes hold of her arm and pulls her back. "Don't touch me unless you mean it," she says. He does, and they spend the night together.

G'Kar has only a moment to recognize Tu'Pari before he fires a gun, and G'Kar is sent sprawling unconscious to the floor. When he wakes up, he has spiky metal contraptions around his neck and wrists. They are paingivers, and as he lunges at Tu'Pari, they spark and crackle, sending pain searing through his body. Tu'Pari tells him he has been instructed to make G'Kar know pain, fear, and then death.

Tu'Pari reaches for his gun as Na'Toth arrives. She

claims to have been sent by the Assassins' Guild as a backup, and to prove it, she viciously kicks G'Kar over and over again, sending him crashing to the back of the room. It is an effective display, but Tu'Pari isn't convinced. In reality, her attack was designed to disable the paingivers, and when Tu'Pari's back is turned, G'Kar rips off the devices. He dives for the assassin with all his anger, lifts him above his head, and throws him hard against the wall. Seventy-two hours later, when Tu'Pari has recovered, G'Kar and Na'Toth send him packing, having ensured that his employers will be out to kill him. "You will know pain," they tell him, "you will know fear . . . and then you will die."

Sinclair leads the ambassadors and command staff into the Central Corridor, where he has chosen to demonstrate Earth's "dominant" belief system. He introduces them to representatives of the various faiths of Earth, who stand in a long line stretching back as far as the eye can see.

"The Parliament of Dreams" takes the opportunity to showcase the different religions and cultures on Babylon 5, while delving a little deeper into some of the characters, particularly Sinclair. It is also the episode that was thrown into panic, when the actress who was supposed to be playing Na'Toth freaked out as soon as she put the makeup on and left the show before setting foot in the studio. The shooting schedule had to be hastily rearranged, while Executive Producer Douglas Netter was on the phone trying to get a replacement actress. At lunchtime he walked in with Julie Caitlin Brown.

"I find it invigorating," says Julie, whose professional name at the time was simply Caitlin Brown. "You walk in, and if you do your homework, you get to create a life for that person. I sat down with Joe Straczynski and said, 'Tell me who she is to you,' then I asked some questions and came up with an answer. I knew there was a possibility of it being offered to me, and my livelihood depended on the fact that I walk in and create something pretty quickly. It's like being on a roller coaster. It's scary—but hey, it's fun!"

In all the panic, Na'Toth's key fight scene had already been filmed using a stunt double, and Julie was just supposed to provide the dialogue. But she is a very physical actress and begged the director to refilm the whole thing. "They said, 'You want to kick this guy?' And I said, 'Yeah,' because I hate it when they cut away and it's obviously not the actor. I got so into it that I kicked the camera! I did this really high kick and just whacked the camera. I thought, 'Oh my God, I've broken this very expensive piece of equipment.' "

Fortunately the camera survived, as did Julie Caitlin Brown, who went on to appear in four subsequent episodes as Na'Toth. Her casting may not have been planned, but it was certainly inspired as she brought a much-needed strength to the character. "Bless Caitlin Brown," says Andreas Katsulas, who plays opposite her as G'Kar. "She took it all on, and that stuff [the makeup] can be so disconcerting. Suddenly, someone who's very animated can become very withdrawn because they feel they can't move. She went with it, and we had a good chemistry. She knew she needed to bring in something strong to work with me."

"The Parliament of Dreams" also takes the opportunity to Humanize Sinclair, taking him away from his duties as the commander of a space station and putting him in a vulnerable situation with Catherine Sakai. Neither of them is comfortable with the relationship, yet it is one they are both drawn to. "I did not want to do the usual hero dashing from woman to woman," says writer Joe Straczynski. "This is a guy who every day handles the hassles and the rigor of this huge station of a quarter of a million people who can't get his relationships to work. I kinda like that. I can relate to that."

The scenes with Sinclair and Catherine were so crucial to expanding the character that the actors, Michael O'Hare and Julia Nickson, spent a lot of time getting the nuances and the subtleties just right. "One of the problems I had in playing the part was there were so many expositional responsibilities in the storytelling. It was really about a guy going around problem solving all the time," says Michael. "I tried to show him as vulnerable as possible to the woman. I stole the idea from the old John Wayne movies, where you would have John Wayne do everything heroically and get all the problems done and as soon as he was on a date he was at a total loss for words, he didn't know what to do."

All this is happening against the background of the religious festival on Babylon 5. The Centauri are the first to showcase their religion with an elaborate banquet inspired by the ancient Roman tradition. "I wanted it to be a Roman banquet just short of an orgy," says director Jim Johnston. "There were dancing girls, there was too much food and too much drink. Londo, of course, had too much to drink. I designed this long dolly shot, and only Peter [Jurasik, playing Londo], the cameraman, and I knew that he was going to get up on the table and crawl down, knocking everything over. I really wanted a fresh reaction from everyone at that table—and I got it."

"It was really about climbing up on the table and going for it," says Peter. "I had Claudia sitting next to me giggling. That's a good one to look back on because Claudia's really funny; we had a great old time together, she and I, during that scene. Mira's face is interesting to watch during that scene; somehow she transcends the Delenn character, and I could see that this fabulous, distinctive, sophisticated actress that she is was staring in horror at this Hollywood actor who was crawling across the table screaming at her. It was a wonderful day on the set, and it continues to be a particularly favorite scene of mine because it was about releasing yourself. You really run the risk of going over the edge, but you can't be afraid of it. You have to go to the edge in order to know where the edge is."

"I thought, 'Let's see how far I can push this,' and it came out wonderfully," says Joe Straczynski. "I was there when we shot that scene, and no one could even breathe they were laughing so hard. I felt for the first time in that episode that we were getting into our stride a little bit. I knew the characters well enough; I knew the actors well enough to know their capabilities; I could play around with it a bit. When I'm not sure about something is when I tend to be the most serious about it. When I get more confident with characters, I tend to get goofier. I say, 'Okay, let's have some fun now.' "

The Centauri banquet shows how decadent their culture has become, in contrast to the Minbari ceremony, which is far more graceful. However, three words were cut from the scene that Joe Straczynski wishes he had kept in. Originally, Delenn's words were "*And Valen said, 'Will you follow me into fire . . .,*' " which would have suggested that Valen was the one who set up the Grey Council. At this time, Delenn had her suspicions of who Sinclair might become, and the way she looks at him while reciting Valen's words suggests that connection. It may have been done unconsciously and unintentionally, but it is there in Mira Furlan's expression. "I found it interesting to do it in—I don't want to exaggerate it—but in a kind of sexy way, a double meaning in swallowing that little thing," she says.

The episode ends by showcasing Earth's religions as Sinclair introduces a long line of representatives from its many faiths. Michael O'Hare describes it as a feat of concentration because he had only half an hour to memorize all the names. "I learned them as much as I possibly could, made a list of them, went over and over them to do that," he says. "Since I was raised a Catholic, I made the second one a Catholic priest, and I gave him my mother's maiden name, Chrisanti—she's part Sicilian—and that's why he's called Father Chrisanti."

It brings together all the disparate religions of Earth in a similar way to Babylon 5's melting pot of alien cultures. "My belief is that we profit from a diversity of voices and a multiplicity of opinions," says Joe Straczynski. "At our best we embrace our differences, and [I wanted] to show that through that last ceremony. Some of the people who were there [playing the religious representatives] were who they appeared to be, and some were not. The rabbi was a biker as a matter of fact—he had tattoos all over his arms! He was scary beforehand. Then they put him in the whole thing, and it was okay."

The scene had 160 extras, adding to the impact, which just wouldn't have been the same with fewer people. "Some of the Warners executives came down to be there on that day," remembers Joe, "and even they were moved by it."

6
"Mind War"

Cast

Commander Jeffrey Sinclair ....Michael O'Hare
Lt. Commander Susan Ivanova ....Claudia Christian
Security Chief Michael Garibaldi ....Jerry Doyle
Ambassador Delenn ....Mira Furlan
Dr. Stephen Franklin ....Richard Biggs
Talia Winters ....Andrea Thompson
Vir Cotto ....Stephen Furst
Lennier ....Bill Mumy
Na'Toth ....Caitlin Brown
Ambassador G'Kar ....Andreas Katsulas
Ambassador Londo Mollari ....Peter Jurasik

Guest Stars

Bester ....Walter Koenig
Jason Ironheart ....William Allan Young
Kelsey ....Felicity Waterman
Catherine Sakai ....Julia Nickson
Earth Fighter ....Don Dowe
Guest Liaison ....Elisa Pensler Gabrielli
Narn Captain ....Michael McKenzie
Businessman ....Kevin Page
Security Guard ....Mark S. Porro
Garibaldi's Aide ....Macaulay Bruton
Dome Tech. No. 1 ....Marianne Robertson

Sinclair stiffens as he senses someone's thoughts in his mind. He looks up to see two figures dressed in black—Psi Cops, highly advanced members of the Psi Corps, who police other telepaths. Bester and his associate, Ms. Kelsey, are on Babylon 5 to track down a rogue telepath. "Our job is to find him and bring him back," he says. "Alive, if possible. Dead, if necessary."

The rogue's name is Jason Ironheart, Talia Winters's former instructor at the Psi Corps Training Academy

*and her lover. Talia insists she hasn't heard from him for
a year, but Bester scans her "to be sure." Talia's hands
clutch at her temples as she feels the Psi Cop burrowing
into her mind. She cries out in pain, then staggers
forward as he lets go. "She's telling the truth," Bester
concludes. "She hasn't seen him."*

*Outside in the corridor, Talia senses someone behind
her. She turns to see Jason Ironheart. He tells her he was
part of a Psi Corps experiment to create a stable
telekinetic with the ability to manipulate matter with
only a thought. But the experiment created a power far
greater than simple telekinesis, and he is determined that
the power should not fall into the hands of the Psi
Corps. "We all thought the Psi Corps was controlled by
the government," he tells her. "But that's changing. The
Corps is starting to pull the strings behind the scenes.
They're more powerful than you can begin to imagine."*

*Catherine Sakai is in her survey ship out by Sigma
957, where a valuable deposit of Quantium 40 is said to
exist. She remembers G'Kar's warning to stay away.
"Sigma 957 is not a healthy place," she intones,
shrugging off his caution as a Narn ploy to keep the
planet for themselves. But moments later a blast of white
light engulfs her ship, and she finds herself facing an
incomprehensible alien craft.*

*Ironheart is changing faster than he anticipated. At
each new level it takes him longer to regain control.
Talia persuades Sinclair that the only way to stop him
from endangering the station is to provide him with a
way out. But before they can get to a ship, the Psi Cops
arrive. Waves of energy crackle across Ironheart's body
as they try to plant a fail-safe code in his mind and shut
him down. "Let him go!" Sinclair bellows at Bester, and
punches him, breaking the telepathic connection. Kelsey
moves in on Ironheart with her PPG trained on him. He
holds out his hand and vaporizes her in an instant.*

*Catherine Sakai's ship is skimming the atmosphere of
Sigma 957 without enough power to resist the gravity,
which is pulling her to her death. Then out of nowhere*

appear two rescue ships. They were sent by G'Kar, who knew what she would encounter. "There are things in the universe billions of years older than either of our races," he says, "and we've learned we can either stay out from underfoot or be stepped on."

Sinclair, Talia, and Ivanova watch in the Observation Dome as Ironheart's ship explodes into a brilliant white glow of energy that swirls into an almost-Humanoid form. "Talia . . . I have become," he whispers. "In memory of love, I give you a gift." A beam of light reaches in and touches Talia. Later, in her quarters, she finds she has a power that she never had before, the ability to move a penny using only her thoughts.

"**M**ind War" was so well received when the episode was finished that it was moved forward in the running order. "It was just one of those shows where everything clicks," says the writer and executive producer, Joe Straczynski. "It was one of our most effects-driven shows from that period, and it brought the Psi Corps into the foreground for the first time. A lot of folks really got off on the Psi Corps. This is a very cool organization, cool in an ominous sort of way, and it hit all the elements of mysticism on the one hand, conspiracies, counterconspiracies, and put Talia in the middle of the story. It had all the elements there to make for a good story for us: the action, the face-off between one person and the larger forces. The performances by all the actors were great. Walter did a terrific job."

The role of Bester was especially written for Walter Koenig because Joe Straczynski felt he had been typecast as Chekov, the character he played in *Star Trek*. Joe had seen some of his other work, particularly in the theater, and he knew he had more to offer. "He wrote not only the things that were very right for my character, but the way that I would say them," says Walter. "I just felt so comfortable with the dialogue that he wrote. And I think the scene which is really the key, to at least part of his personality, was established in that episode when I say, 'Anatomically impossible, Mr. Garibaldi, but you're welcome to try.' It was the delivery that gave me a key to how the character was to be played."

Bester proved so popular and so intriguing that his character continued to show up in *Babylon 5* and Walter became a semiregular member of the cast. But this was not the original plan. He was originally slated to play the one-off character Knight Two in "And the Sky Full of Stars" but, in a bizarre twist of fate, was forced to pull out through illness. "Things have a strange way of happening, don't they?" he says.

It was also a key episode for Talia, as her former lover Jason Ironheart arrives on Babylon 5, revealing an emotional side of the character that hadn't been seen before and forcing her into conflict with the Psi Corps. "It was really wonderful for me," says Andrea Thompson (Talia). "It was the first glimpse I had had of Talia's past and the depth that she was capable of. You saw a little bit more of Talia, and she wasn't the ice queen that she appeared to be in the beginning. It was just a magnificent episode for me, and I wrote Joe a note and sent him coffee and chocolates after that because it was one of those episodes I will remember for the rest of my life."

One of the most powerful moments for Talia is when she submits to Bester's telepathic scan in a scene that reveals both her vulnerability and the tyranny of the Psi Cops. "I envisioned it as a rape of sorts," says Andrea. "It's a rape of the mind and not of the body, which has got to be even more horrifying, although I have never gone through anything like that. As an actor you just think of all the most painful experiences of your life—which in my experience is childbirth and root canal—and try to combine them with the horrifying idea of what it would be like to have someone crawl into your mind against your will. And what I tried to put across at the very end of the scene was her sense of humiliation."

It culminated in the scene in the Zocalo where the Psi Cops confront Talia and Sinclair (Michael O'Hare) as they are leading Ironheart on an escape route to the docking bay. As often happens with an action scene, it was a very technical piece to film because of the involvement of special effects, the use of a wind machine, flying sparks, and a metal beam falling from the ceiling. "It is very choreographed," says Andrea. "When we were first shooting it, it was quite funny because the beam came down—these things are made of Styrofoam; a baby could pick them up—and Michael stepped right through it! You could see that it actually *was* Styrofoam. He went crashing right through the beam!"

There was an extra moment added to this scene that wasn't in the script. Talia wasn't originally supposed to do anything when Ironheart was being threatened by the second Psi Cop, and Andrea thought this was unrealistic. The point when she reaches toward him and is thrown back by his energy was her idea. "I had to fight for that moment," she remembers. "I said, 'Here's the love of her life, and they're attacking him, and she's not going to jump in there?' And then they said, 'No, she wouldn't because she knows she'll be killed.' But I said, 'Don't you realize love overcomes all that? You don't even *think* of that if it is love.' If it was Jerry and there were three guys with guns, I'd jump in front of him. I mean that's what love is."

It was Andrea's real-life relationship with her fellow actor Jerry Doyle that also provided the inspiration for the way she handled the scene at the end, when Ironheart gives her the gift of telekinesis. "You know what it reminded me of when we were doing that scene? When I first found out that Jerry and I were expecting. It's a magical gift, but at the same time, you're terribly afraid. It's all about the unknown, and you have that sense that your life is changing, that something has happened, you can never turn back."

Talia's extra powers clearly laid the foundation for upcoming storylines in *Babylon 5*, but all that was lost when Andrea Thompson left the show at the end of the second season. Joe Straczynski admits he had plans for her powers but refuses to elaborate further. "There were anticipations of possibilities," he says cryptically, "but like the college student who wins a scholarship to the best university and then crosses the street and gets hit by a bus, possibilities don't always equal realities."

A different part of the arc that was mentioned here and later becomes much more significant is the idea of the First Ones, races much older than Humanity. Catherine Sakai encounters one such race at Sigma 957 and survives only because G'Kar sends out a couple of ships to save her. It was quite an unexpected turn for the character G'Kar, who, up to this point, had been seen more as a warlike figure. "That really fuddled a lot of fans who felt sure he was the bad guy, which I loved," says Joe. "I really saw Londo moving around, but I hadn't really moved G'Kar much, and this was a chance to begin doing that with his character."

G'Kar compares Catherine Sakai's position in the face of the ancient race to that of an ant that has no way to comprehend what has happened to it when he picks it up on the tip of his glove. "That was a hallmark episode," says Andreas Katsulas (G'Kar). "I talk a lot about this character having all these dimensions that I can't normally play outside of *Babylon 5*, and this was one of the perfect examples of what I mean. This man, this character, alien, mysterious, passionate, is suddenly talking about an ant. He has a side that contemplates the universe. All the façades are taken away as he becomes interested in one curious phenomenon. It's so touching, it moves me."

G'Kar's comment that he is both terrified and reassured that there are still wonders in the universe was very much the message Joe Straczynski was trying to convey. "Too often in television science fiction shows, going to a different planet is treated with all the wonder and expectation of going to the corner 7-Eleven," he says. "SF is the literature of wonder; to me that is the core of science fiction. Things aren't all driven by science and us knowing all the answers. There are still mysteries out there, and when the mysteries are gone, that's when you've got to pack it in because there is nothing left to do."

7

"The War Prayer"

Cast

Commander Jeffrey Sinclair ....Michael O'Hare
Lt. Commander Susan Ivanova ....Claudia Christian
Security Chief Michael Garibaldi ....Jerry Doyle
Ambassador Delenn ....Mira Furlan
Dr. Stephen Franklin ....Richard Biggs
Talia Winters ....Andrea Thompson
Vir Cotto ....Stephen Furst
Lennier ....Bill Mumy
Na'Toth ....Caitlin Brown
Ambassador G'Kar ....Andreas Katsulas
Ambassador Londo Mollari ....Peter Jurasik

Guest Stars

Malcolm Biggs ....Tristan Rogers
Shaal Mayan ....Nancy Lee Grahn
Roberts ....Michael Paul Chan
Kiron Maray ....Rodney Eastman
Aria Tensus ....Danica McKellar
Mila Shar ....Diane Adair
Alvares ....Richard Chaves
Thegras ....Mark Hendrickson
Security Officer No. 1 ....Chuck Butto
Kosh ....Ardwright Chamberlain
Alien No. 1 ....Mike Gunther
Dome Tech ....Marianne Robertson

The Minbari poet Mayan turns as she hears the sound of steel scraping against steel in the dark corridors of Babylon 5. A figure moves out of the shadows and stabs her. She cries out in pain and collapses to the floor, where her assailant stamps a mark on her smooth Minbari forehead. "Stay away from Earth, freak!" he says, and is gone.

Ivanova is in the Customs Area, where two young Centauris have been arrested for using stolen credit chips. As she orders a Centauri representative be informed, a man catches her eye. His name is Malcolm Biggs, the man she left eight years ago so she could concentrate on her career.

The two young Centauris, Aria and Kiron, are placed in Londo's care. He has no sympathy for their position. They have run away from home because their families want them to enter into arranged marriages, while they want to marry each other for love. "Love?" he scoffs. "What has love got to do with marriage?"

Aria and Kiron meet under the soft light of night emanating from the station's core. They skip down the corridor to a bench, where they kiss. Out of the darkness emerge three figures, and Aria screams as a PPG blast strikes Kiron in the chest. She goes to him, but a shock stick sends a bolt of pain through her stomach, and she collapses unconscious on the ground next to him.

"We can no longer stand idly by as our peoples are slaughtered by these cowardly Humans," G'Kar cries to a mob of aliens who have gathered in the Zocalo. Eight non-Humans have been attacked within the past two weeks and unrest is building. The attacks were almost certainly the work of the Homeguard, a pro-Earth group opposed to alien involvement in what they consider to be Human affairs. Garibaldi eventually manages to catch one of the leaders on a surveillance tape, trying to recruit a new member—it is Malcolm Biggs, Ivanova's former lover.

Sinclair convinces Biggs that he, too, is a pro-Earth sympathizer, and Biggs sets up a meeting with the Homeguard in the cargo bay. Biggs tests Sinclair's loyalty by throwing an Abbai woman at his feet and offering him a PPG. "Kill it," he says. Sinclair hesitates as the alien begs for mercy.

Scanners detect Garibaldi's men approaching. It

*distracts Biggs for a second, and Sinclair takes his
chance, grabbing the PPG and punching Biggs in the
face. Sinclair and Ivanova dive for cover as an exchange
of PPG blasts crisscrosses the cargo bay. Biggs sneaks
behind Sinclair and trains his weapon on him, but
Ivanova is there before he can fire. "I wouldn't," she
says, aiming her PPG at him. "Give me an excuse, and
you're dead."*

*Vir thinks Londo is wrong to insist that Aria and
Kiron must go through with their arranged marriages
and plucks up the courage to tell him so. Londo's
response is not what he expected. "My shoes are too
tight, but it doesn't matter because I have forgotten how
to dance," Londo says, remembering what his father
told him many years ago. Realizing that these words
now apply to himself, he makes arrangements for Aria
and Kiron to be able to choose whom they will marry
when they are old enough. When Kiron asks why, Londo
tells them, "Because you are still children, and children
should be allowed to dance."*

"The War Prayer" introduces the Homeguard and
extends the idea of antialien feeling, which is growing
back on Earth. It puts Babylon 5—a station where Humans
and aliens are thrust together in a five-mile-long enclosure of
spinning metal—at the center of the controversy. It had
already been established that many people didn't think
Babylon 5 would survive, particularly after the destruction
or disappearance of Babylons 1 to 4. Many also thought it
was a waste of money and resources, that after the Earth–
Minbari War Humanity should be looking inward at its own
problems. Such has been the argument that has dictated
many examples of foreign policy in the twentieth century.

When Malcolm Biggs complains of "alien ambassadors
setting policy for Humans, alien workers taking jobs away
from Human beings, inhuman criminals preying on decent
people," he is echoing sentiments that have sparked conflicts throughout our own history, whether based on racial,

social, religious, or nationalistic prejudice. It is a potential flashpoint on Babylon 5 and is opened up when aliens start being attacked by pro-Earth extremists and respond with anti-Human feeling of their own.

The three main plots interweave themselves over the background of the Homeguard and bounce the themes of love and tolerance off each other. The script was written by D. C. Fontana from a premise supplied by Joe Straczynski. They talked a great deal about the episode and the show in general before she started, because, at this early stage, there was only the pilot episode available for reference. "I was in touch with Joe, asking him questions about the series, because when a show is just getting started, it's hard to know everything that's going on," says Dorothy Fontana. "You don't know who the actors are yet, and you haven't met them, and you don't know how they sound, the way they phrase things, or their delivery. So he sent me a whole lot of completed scripts, and that started to give me a handle on the relationships of all the characters."

Joe Straczynski's original premise centered mostly around the arrival of Ivanova's former lover, Malcolm Biggs, and was, as Dorothy recalls, fairly sketchy. "It was about a page, maybe three-quarters of a page, outlining the relationship between Ivanova and the man," she says. "I was trying to explore a little bit about Ivanova and find out a little bit more about her. I had seen Claudia Christian in one other thing, which was not Babylon 5, but it was still hard to know who she was at that point. The thing was, it was a relatively stock situation, and you kind of knew what had to happen, but on the other hand, I think that Claudia came off very well and interesting as a character."

Claudia Christian is not so sure. "It was probably interesting to see that she would be attracted to a guy like that, but I didn't see anything particularly Ivanova-ish about her choice with him. Maybe he was such a jerk that she ended up with Talia because of complete embarrassment!"

The relationship allowed Ivanova to get out of Command and Control and out of her uniform, revealing she is a woman who has the capacity to love, to smile, and to laugh, but the overwhelming impression is that she is a woman very much dedicated to her duty. "There were a lot of complaints, of course, that I was too stiff in the beginning," says Claudia, "but my response was always that I was new and that's how you act when you're new in the job. You're a little intimidated and by the book. So I think your personality starts to show the more comfortable you feel someplace, the more confident you become."

Ivanova's romantic relationship is juxtaposed with that of the two young Centauri lovers who come aboard Babylon 5 seeking refuge from their parents' marriage plans. This plot thread didn't come out of the original premise, but was introduced by Dorothy Fontana. "Joe said, 'Well, I don't want them to be young lovers,' " she remembers, "and I said, 'Well, it's not really about young lovers: it's about Londo and what is happening in his life.' So it's really more of a character study on him and how this situation involves him and brings him out as a character."

It shows Londo as rather a sad figure, who feels there is no place for love in the great Centauri tradition. He says that, in order to keep the Centauri Republic strong, noble houses are melded together by the institution of marriage, and this demands great sacrifice. For him, it has meant being married to three women, whom he calls Pestilence, Famine, and Death. At first he demands that the youngsters should also follow that tradition and is ready to send them back home. Later he comes to realize that it would only condemn them to a life like his own, a life without love. It culminates in the speech in which he remembers his father's words: "My shoes are too tight, but it doesn't matter because I have forgotten how to dance." He is suddenly in the same position as his father, looking back at his life and realizing he has forsaken happiness for tradition. That is a legacy, he decides, he cannot pass on to the next generation.

The speech was added to the episode by Joe Straczynski and became one of the most powerful of the season. One of the reasons it makes such an impact is Peter Jurasik's emotional performance, and yet the actor feels he did not do justice to the material. "A beautiful speech," he says: "I really felt like I was starting to feel a stride in the higher tones for Londo, but I never really found that speech. It's a tough episode for me to watch, because I felt that Joe wrote some important stuff. I don't know how I fit in the scheme with other actors, but more often than not, you will find me standing at Joe's door just knocking—'Er, Joe, what does this mean?' and 'Why am I doing this?'—and he'll very patiently, like a good father, explain to me. So either I didn't get it intellectually or I just didn't get there emotionally, which is probably more the case. So I don't think the script was in any way realized. The wonderful thing about Joe's lines is they will sometimes support you, and you can do an okay mediocre performance, and like a surfer, you can lay back on the wave and the good line will pick you up and bring you into shore."

Another addition to the episode picked up on something hanging over from the pilot. There had been much discussion about how the assassin could have poisoned Kosh with a skin tab when he would have been protected within his encounter suit. This very same thought occurs to Sinclair in "The War Prayer," and he mentions it to Ivanova. The two scenes were originally filmed for "The Parliament of Dreams" but were moved when "Parliament" came out too long. "What we tend to do is keep threads alive," says Joe Straczynski. "That kind of thing is going to come up later on. We let the viewers know that we haven't forgotten these things and that eventually this will have to get brought up in some way or another. The best way of doing it is just to mention it once in a while and say, 'You know it's here, we know it's here, and we haven't forgotten about it.' "

So is it finally resolved? "Yes and no," says Joe. "That he was willing to reveal himself, we find out later on that what we see is not what there actually is, so in a way it does resolve it."

The episode has an important role to play in advancing the story, not only with the discussion of the nature of the Vorlons, but also with the introduction of the Homeguard and the political problems back on Earth. However, where it mostly succeeds is in the way it expands many of the characters. Delenn gets the opportunity to meet with an old friend and reminisce about her youth. It softens Ivanova as she is reacquainted with an old boyfriend. Vir takes a great leap in confidence when he stands up to Londo for the first time, telling him he is wrong about the Centauri lovers, and Londo responds to that by revealing he has a heart after all.

8

"And the Sky Full of Stars"

Cast

Commander Jeffrey Sinclair ....Michael O'Hare
Lt. Commander Susan Ivanova ....Claudia Christian
Security Chief Michael Garibaldi ....Jerry Doyle
Ambassador Delenn ....Mira Furlan
Dr. Stephen Franklin ....Richard Biggs
Talia Winters ....Andrea Thompson
Vir Cotto ....Stephen Furst
Lennier ,...Bill Mumy
Na'Toth ....Caitlin Brown
Ambassador G'Kar ....Andreas Katsulas
Ambassador Londo Mollari ....Peter Jurasik

Guest Stars

Knight One ....Judson Scott
Knight Two ....Christopher Neame
Benson ....Jim Youngs
Mitchell ....Justin Williams
Guard ....Joe Banks
Strongarm No. 1 ....Gary Cervantes
Grey Council No. 1 .... Mark Hendrickson
Security Guard ....Fumi Shishino
Aide ....Macaulay Bruton
Tech. No. 1 ....Marianne Robertson

"I've identified the target," Knight One says, inserting a data crystal into a holographic projector. It emits a flash of light, and an image is thrown into the center of the room—the image is of Commander Sinclair.

Sinclair is sleeping in his quarters. Dreaming. Remembered images pass through his mind. He is in the cockpit of his ship at the Battle of the Line, the final

*battle of the Earth–Minbari War. A shadow falls across
his face. He looks up and finds himself staring directly at
a Minbari war cruiser. The shock is enough to wake him
into consciousness.*

*Sinclair is back in his quarters. He tries to access his
computer. Nothing happens. He tries to call
maintenance. Nothing. He gets dressed and walks
through empty corridor after empty corridor to the
Observation Dome. It is deserted. He tries the main
console repeatedly until it eventually comes on-line. It
tells him there is only one other life-form on board—in
the Central Corridor.*

*A voice calls from above him in the darkened
corridor, and Knight Two steps out of the shadows.
"Your mind is in here with me," he says, placing his
hand to his temple. It is all a simulation, a Virtual
Reality Cybernet that exists only in Sinclair's mind and
the mind of Knight Two.*

*"We're finally going to get to the truth," says the
Knight. He doesn't believe Sinclair's story that he tried to
ram the Minbari cruiser and then blacked out for
twenty-four hours, waking up after the Minbari had
surrendered and the war was over. Sinclair says he can't
remember what happened in those missing twenty-four
hours. "I've never been able to remember."*

*The Knights turn up the power of the Cybernet and
push Sinclair harder. What happened at the Battle of
the Line? Why did the Minbari surrender on the eve of
their victory? Did they decide it was easier to infiltrate
Earth from within, using people like Sinclair as their
agents? Sinclair insists he never betrayed Earth, but
how can he be sure? He flashes back to the moment a
Minbari told him, "There is a hole in your mind." Back
then, it was enough to make him wonder about those
twenty-four hours, and now it is enough for Knight
Two to take him back and make him relive the missing time.*

The Minbari cruiser catches him in a tractor beam

and pulls his ship inside. He is strung up on a metal
frame, bleeding and in shock. Another flash and he is
standing in the center of a circle of grey-cloaked figures.
He approaches one of them and pulls back its grey hood.
He recognizes the face underneath. It is Delenn.

Sinclair flexes his arm and pulls himself out of the
Cybernet. He is back in reality, back on Babylon 5, but
as he grabs a PPG and staggers into the corridor, his
mind is still on board the Minbari cruiser. He sees grey
figures instead of people, and he is so delusional he fires
on Garibaldi. Then Delenn—ignoring all of Garibaldi's
warnings to stay back—approaches him. He sees her
face, listens to her calming voice, and is brought back to
his senses.

Back in his quarters, Sinclair reflects on what he has
seen. He knows now that the Minbari blanked his
memory before they surrendered and then let him go.
"What is it they don't want me to remember?" he asks
himself. "I have to find out."

"It's one of my favorite episodes," says Michael O'Hare, and it's easy to see why. The episode concentrates almost entirely on his character, Sinclair, and delves deep into his own pain and frustration over the missing twenty-four hours of his life. It was set up in "The Gathering," and only here, eight episodes into the first season, does it start to pay off. It does so by using the concept of virtual reality in a way that not only takes the audience back to the time of the battle, but also allows them to see it from Sinclair's perspective eleven years ago.

"I didn't just want to talk about the battle: I wanted to see what happened," says Joe Straczynski. "To have a person sitting at the bar with his feet on the table saying, 'and then we went up to the ship . . .' [wouldn't have worked]. I wanted them to relive it and see it. Therefore, somebody had to push him into seeing it all again. Given that he has probably tried for a long time to remember what happened and hasn't been able to, it required an outside agency to force the issue, hence the two Knights and the virtual-reality environment."

The look of the episode is part of its success, convincing the audience they are inside Sinclair's mind through the use of darkened sets highlighted with spotlights and a feeling of claustrophobia that increases as the interrogation intensifies. Part of the credit for that must go to the director, Janet Greek, who was asked to develop a look for *Babylon 5* with her first episode, "And the Sky Full of Stars." "I wanted to have a feeling that we're in a universal void," she says. "So I asked for lighting which was spotlit in the area I was working in and for everything else to fall off into darkness. And believe me, for somebody who works in television, I know there is not a DP [director of photography] in the world that wouldn't do that without being hysterically nervous. But I talked to John Flinn [the DP] before I did that; we really talked about a lighting style for the show, and so when we came to it, it worked out really well."

Janet Greek consciously took a theatrical approach when staging the scenes, which fitted Joe Straczynski's writing style and enhanced the distinctive feel of the episode. "It allowed me to do a more geometrical staging with everything," says Janet. "It was just really the bodies and the lights and nothing else."

The casting of the Englishman Christopher Neame as Knight Two also complemented the theatrical approach. "He's a wonderful actor," says Michael O'Hare. "He was great fun to work with. One of the things I loved about the show is I got a chance to work with a lot of Englishmen, and I love English actors."

The interrogation scenes between Sinclair and Knight Two are central to "And the Sky Full of Stars." On one level they are teasing out information about the Battle of the Line and, on another level, exploring Sinclair's guilt that he survived when so many others died. Knight Two hits at the heart of Sinclair's guilt when he says he hides behind duty, obligation, and responsibility. "Sinclair is a wounded bird," says Joe, "and by putting him under this pressure, you can crack away the exterior he usually uses to keep people at a distance or to present a controlled exterior. One thing that I try to do every so often in the show is to take a nonlinear or surrealistic approach to something. In the first part you don't know what the hell is going on—why is the station so empty? I wanted the character to be totally disoriented. An interrogator will tell you that part of breaking down the personality is to disorient the person. I wanted to see what happens when you peel Sinclair's mask away and see what's inside, the fractured personality."

For Michael O'Hare, it was the chance to give a little more depth to his character. This was one time when using something from his own experience helped him get a handle on the character's situation. "As far as the underpinning of the scenes was concerned, I understood them very well from things in my private life," he says. "I understood what the experience was of losing everything, having everything taken away from me."

It is even more pronounced when Sinclair is remembering his military experiences, and it is the main reason why Michael likes the episode so much. "I have two brothers who are in the U.S. Navy. One flies on F14 jet planes that take off and land on aircraft carriers—he's a lieutenant—and the other one's a captain, who's in charge of building aircraft carriers in America. I think that people in the States and here [the U.K.], for what it's worth, are too hard on their military people and not appreciative enough of them. Those who are in the military who are fascist pigs, I don't like any more than anybody else does, but most of the people have a tendency to be a very good sort, very noble, really care about God and country. And there's a moment in that episode where I talk about everyone dying in front of me, and I really did that as a tribute to my brothers and the fact that what they do for a living involves the threat of loss of the most complete kind."

Perhaps that is why some of the flashbacks to the Battle of the Line are so powerful, as Sinclair watches a sky full of stars, each star an exploding ship signaling the death of another one of his colleagues. "When we were shooting the battle scenes, I suggested to the director: 'Why don't you have the lights come from different places?' " says Michael. "So that the audience watches him turn and see another comrade killed, turn again and see another comrade killed, and then another one. That was my idea. It brings home to the audience that everyone's dying."

The flashbacks eventually push Sinclair into remembering being taken aboard the Minbari cruiser and being tortured by the Grey Council. "All I can say is that when the Minbari interrogate you, they can be awfully rough," says Michael O'Hare with a smile.

The purpose of this, of course, is to deepen the mystery by revealing that Delenn was part of the Minbari ruling body that ended the war by surrendering after they interrogated Sinclair. "Whenever I look at exposition, I try to figure out ways of passing it along so it doesn't feel like exposition," says Joe Straczynski. "I try and make sure that every scene does two things, and that was a chance not only to show his [Sinclair's] background but also to put her [Delenn] in a position in the Grey Council."

"We see that there is a completely different trait to her, which is almost a military leader," says Mira Furlan, who plays Delenn. "We discover that she's something else besides being this gentle spiritual soul. I prefer her as a pacifist, but that's just my own state of mind."

When Sinclair eventually breaks out of the Cybernet, he is still hallucinating. This helped add an extra layer to the distinctive look of the episode and another challenge. "They actually had more hallucinatory effects in the script than they used," Michael remembers. "Every time he heard a sound [it was supposed to echo around his mind]. I played that, but they didn't technically back it up."

"That was difficult for Michael," says the director, Janet Greek. "But he did a good job with them. We fooled around with how to do all that stuff. It was a very experimental episode in many ways, and it was different from so many things that have been done on television. It's the episode that I remember the most vividly, and it's not just that it was my first one. It was so beautifully written and well thought out and so unusual. I loved it."

The episode ends having answered many of the questions surrounding Sinclair's experience at the Battle of the Line. But in doing so, it poses larger questions that set up more possibilities for future episodes and become more significant as the story progresses.

9
"Deathwalker"

Cast

Commander Jeffrey Sinclair ....Michael O'Hare
Lt. Commander Susan Ivanova ....Claudia Christian
Security Chief Michael Garibaldi ....Jerry Doyle
Ambassador Delenn ....Mira Furlan
Dr. Stephen Franklin ....Richard Biggs
Talia Winters ....Andrea Thompson
Vir Cotto ....Stephen Furst
Lennier ....Bill Mumy
Na'Toth ....Caitlin Brown
Ambassador G'Kar ....Andreas Katsulas
Ambassador Londo Mollari ....Peter Jurasik

Guest Stars

Jha'dur ....Sarah Douglas
Ambassador Kalika ....Robin Curtis
Abbut ....Cosie Costa
Senator Hidoshi ....Aki Aleong
Kosh ....Ardwright Chamberlain
Ambassador No. 1 ....Robert DiTillio
Tech. No. 2 ....Sav Farrow
Ashok ....Mark Hendrickson
Tech. No. 1 ....Marianne Robertson

"Deathwalker!" screams Na'Toth, racing through the customs hall to grab the woman she has seen walking in. Na'Toth slams her up against some packing cases, tearing at her flesh, beating her savagely, until security guards pull her away, still screaming.

Deathwalker is the name given to the war criminal Jha'dur, who wiped out entire races, destroyed whole planets, and experimented on living beings. She infected the entire population of Lardec 4 with Stafford's Disease just to see how long it would take them to die. Na'Toth's family was among those who suffered at her hands, and

*they have pledged revenge. But, muses Sinclair, if the
woman really was Deathwalker, she would be an old
woman by now.*

*Talia Winters has been employed by Ambassador
Kosh to sit in on some negotiations he is holding with a
strange man in a large hat named Abbut. Kosh asks her
to scan Abbut, but she can sense no thoughts at all. "It's
as if his mind were empty," she says.*

*The woman Na'Toth attacked is Deathwalker, kept
youthful by an anti-agapic drug she has developed. She
came to Babylon 5 to negotiate with the Narns about
her discovery, but Earth also wants her immortality
serum, regardless of her war-crimes record. "Justice or
immortality," comments Ivanova, "an intriguing
choice."*

*Kosh's negotiations with Abbut make no sense. They
keep talking in riddles, and Talia can't pick up anything
from Abbut's mind, until . . . Flash! Her mind is hit by
an image of herself standing inside a circle of mirrors,
looking at her own reflection. Flash! She is surrounded
by electronic circuitry, buzzing and sparking with
activity. Flash! She is in a darkened corridor,
approaching a man who reaches out to attack her in the
darkness. She cries out and snaps back to reality. Abbut
lifts his hat to reveal a cyberorganic brain and a data
crystal where he had been recording her thoughts. He
hands the data crystal to Kosh. Talia demands to know
what is on it, and he tells her, "Reflection, surprise,
terror . . . for the future."*

*Sinclair is ordered to send Deathwalker to Earth, but
his resolve to get her off the station quietly is blocked by
the League of Non-Aligned Worlds, demanding
retribution. Others have also heard she is on board, and
their ships are lining up outside Babylon 5 as they insist
that Jha'dur be handed over to them for trial. Sinclair
makes a deal with the League of Non-Aligned Worlds to
allow their scientists to join with Earth experts to
develop Jha'dur's discovery and then turn her over to the
League for trial.*

Jha'dur doesn't believe the Earth Alliance will honor Sinclair's agreement and mocks those who believe they are not capable of the horrors she committed. She believes her drug will change all that because the key element has to be taken from living beings. "For one to live forever, another must die. You will fall upon one another like wolves," she tells Sinclair. "Not like us? You will become us."

A crowd gathers to watch Deathwalker being shipped off the station. But before her ship can leave Babylon 5 space, a Vorlon ship appears out of the jumpgate. It fires, and with one direct hit, the ship explodes, destroying Jha'dur and her serum. "You are not ready for immortality," says Kosh.

"If Hitler came back, how would we react?" That was the premise behind "Deathwalker." The story editor, Lawrence G. DiTillio, was simply told that the episode would involve a notorious war criminal whom Sinclair would defend when she came to Babylon 5. "The thing is, why would Sinclair, who is a very compassionate man, defend such a heinous person?" Larry DiTillio remembers asking himself when he was handed the premise. "I had to come up with a reason, and the only reason I could really come up with was she had the key to immortality, which I thought was actually a pretty good motivation."

His first thought was that it was a fairly standard premise for science fiction, but he began to get excited when he realized the implications for Sinclair. "Sinclair hated this woman, but she's got to be defended because she may be able to atone for what she did. He saw it that way. She killed millions, but she may save billions. Where do we draw the line on knocking her off? Eventually, Sinclair ended up a god, and it kind of showed that godlike streak in him, above petty judgments. He was thinking of a higher purpose all along."

Sinclair finds himself caught in the middle of alien races who are baying for revenge and others who want to get their hands on Deathwalker's immortality serum, including his own government. It is indicative of Sinclair's position as a soldier trying to be a peacemaker that his loyalties are constantly being compromised. On the one hand he is loyal to Earth, but he also has to obey his own conscience and act in the interests of the station: "I think that's very often the case with leadership," says Michael O'Hare. "Often one finds oneself involved in a leadership position which is more visceral initially and deals with life-and-death problems . . . I think it's a good idea to show someone walking the balance and dealing with the frustrations of handling something in a civilian, diplomatic way. You're still dealing with an awful lot of dishonesty and manipulation, and you don't have a lot of the benefits that you have with the military in cutting through the bullshit to the truth."

In this situation his first thought is to obey orders and send Deathwalker to Earth, where the authorities are better equipped to deal with her. But when the League of Non-Aligned Worlds discover his plans, they stop him, and Sinclair is forced to deal with the issue on Babylon 5. From that moment it becomes an internal struggle for him. Not only does he have to juggle the demands of the various alien races, he has to look within himself to find a solution that satisfies everyone. It is one of the controversial decisions that come back to haunt him in "Eyes."

It is also a very personal battle for Na'Toth, whose family was persecuted by Deathwalker. Her account of her grandfather's horrific death makes Deathwalker's atrocities more immediate than the genocide of faceless millions. "I believe in that," says Larry DiTillio. "I believe as much as you can personalize a conflict, it makes for better drama. Everything was very personal. It was always a big scale, but it was always very personal for the people involved."

While this serves the plot, it also adds to the strength of Na'Toth's character. As soon as she sees Deathwalker, she is out to obey her Chon'Kar, or blood oath, and revenge what Jha'dur did to her family. "When I attacked Deathwalker, I felt I was doing everyone a service," says Julie Caitlin Brown, who plays Na'Toth. "It was the whole Jewish

Holocaust question, so she felt very justified in her violence. I don't think she would have chosen violence just walking down the street. She wasn't a violent person, but she was a person who would defend her honor. She would defend her family."

Na'Toth would probably have killed her, if it hadn't been for the security guards and Deathwalker's anti-agapic drug. This was Na'Toth's second major fight in as many episodes, and it shows the physicality that has always been a part of G'Kar's assistant. Even with Ko'Dath, the attaché who met with an unfortunate airlock accident after only one episode, there was a violent streak. "It was always Joe's intention that she would be very physical," Julie explains. "G'Kar's whole energy was that he wasn't a warrior anymore: he was a statesman, and Na'Toth comes into it with a bit of contempt for him. She saw him as someone who messed around with Earth women and wasn't really interested in the cause anymore. Basically, I was brought in to point that difference out. Here's a female that's tougher than G'Kar."

Na'Toth is reined in by her ambassador, even though she is anxious to enact her revenge, no matter what the consequences might be. In the finished episode, his promise that she will eventually be allowed to fulfill her Chon'Kar is enough to keep her restrained until the Vorlons blow up Deathwalker's ship. But in an earlier version of the script, the Na'Toth story thread was developed further. When G'Kar realizes Narn cannot have the immortality serum, he decides that no one should be allowed to have it and releases Na'Toth to confront Deathwalker. Deathwalker is prepared for her, defeats Na'Toth, and is at the point of killing her when Sinclair bursts in and saves her life. These scenes were cut because of time constraints.

"The other thing that 'Deathwalker' did was to put together the League of Non-Aligned Worlds," adds Larry DiTillio. "The whole first season was giving the audience a lot of background to the station before we got into the bigger arc story. Before, we had seen them as background aliens moving across the landscape. When we got to 'Deathwalker,' we were dealing with them by putting them under the one played by Robin Curtis [Kalika, the Abbai ambassador], and we got a little more background."

Woven in throughout the "Deathwalker" plot was Kosh's incomprehensible negotiations with the cyberorganic Vicker, Abbut. They turn out to have been a setup for Kosh to record parts of Talia Winters's mind "for the future." "That was the most bizarre episode, wasn't it?" says the actress Andrea Thompson. "The whole time I was shooting it, I was saying, 'What the hell am I talking about?' It was really an amazing riddle. I was in the dark the whole time I was doing it. Sometimes it's frustrating while you're shooting something like that, because you want to have more knowledge of what you're doing, but in the end it turned out to be a real boon, because the confusion was real. I didn't have to play any of it. I was just as much in the dark as Talia was."

"For us it was just fun," says Larry DiTillio, who wrote the scenes in the belief that the Vicker would be played by Gilbert Gottfried, an actor with a fondness for science fiction and horror. Unfortunately, he was unavailable because he was in New York, and Cosie Costa took on the role instead. "To give Cosie credit, he did his best, but his lines were written for Gilbert Gottfried's cadence. Had he played the part, I think it would have been four times as funny and very weird, because Gottfried is a very weird person."

The existence of the data crystal was clearly a setup for later on, but it was never really used. The memory of the serial killer that Talia scanned on Mars was referred to in "The Quality of Mercy," when she was again asked to scan a killer, but Kosh's plans for the data crystal were never revealed. "Later on it might have been used if Andrea had not left the show," says Larry. "We might have seen her reflection and stuff like that, but we never had the time."

The whole matter of the data crystal is dispensed with in Season Two's "Divided Loyalties," when Talia is revealed to be a spy. Garibaldi says it may be useful to protect them from Talia's uncovered personality, but it does little more than tie up loose ends. It may have something to do with Joe Straczynski's dislike of the Talia Winters subplot in "Deathwalker." "That one was a Larry construct that I really wasn't that happy with," he says. "I didn't care for the Vicker. I wasn't sure I wanted that technology in my universe, and after it was put in, I thought, 'I'm never going to see this ever again'—they all died!"

Despite that small reservation, he is generally pleased with the episode. "It was a successful episode," he says. "It was probably one of the fan favorites for a while."

10
"Believers"

Cast

Commander Jeffrey Sinclair ....Michael O'Hare
Lt. Commander Susan Ivanova ....Claudia Christian
Security Chief Michael Garibaldi ....Jerry Doyle
Ambassador Delenn ....Mira Furlan
Dr. Stephen Franklin ....Richard Biggs
Talia Winters ....Andrea Thompson
Vir Cotto ....Stephen Furst
Lennier ....Bill Mumy
Na'Toth ....Caitlin Brown
Ambassador G'Kar ....Andreas Katsulas
Ambassador Londo Mollari ....Peter Jurasik

Guest Stars

M'ola ....Tricia O'Neil
Tharg ....Stephen Lee
Dr. Maya Hernandez ....Silvana Gallardo
Shon ....Jonathan Charles Kaplan
Kosh ....Ardwright Chamberlain

"Am I going to die?" asks Shon.

Shon is a young alien child brought to Babylon 5 by his devoted parents, who have been told by their own doctors that there is no cure for his watery breathing and he will soon die. Franklin assures them he can save the boy with a simple operation, but the parents forbid it. "The chosen of God must not be punctured," says his mother.

The starliner Asimov *is in trouble. A fire has put its navigational computer out of action, and its route to Babylon 5 takes it through Raider territory. Ivanova, driven stir-crazy by being stuck in the Observation Dome, persuades Sinclair to let her take out a fighter wing and escort the* Asimov *back to base.*

Meanwhile, Shon's parents continue to refuse surgery

because their religion teaches that it will destroy the boy's spirit. Franklin suggests a different procedure that may give the child's body a chance to heal itself. It is a lie, which he hopes will give the parents time to reconsider, but as Shon's condition worsens and they remain steadfast, he appeals to Sinclair.

The parents, frightened by the prospect of being overruled by Earth, turn to the alien ambassadors for help. G'Kar declines because he does not think an alliance with their world would be of advantage to Narn; Londo turns them down because of the cost; Kosh refuses because "the avalanche has already started"; and Delenn says the Minbari will not take sides in a matter of belief. Sinclair knows that if he rules against the parents it will send out a message that Babylon 5 ignores the concerns of other races when it suits Earth. So he refuses to intervene.

Shon struggles with each breath, trying to keep death at bay. Franklin stares at the dying child and decides he doesn't care what Commander Sinclair says: he is going to operate anyway. He holds the knife over Shon's unconscious body and hesitates for a moment. "You can't help but wonder, can you?" says his assistant, Dr. Hernandez. He says a prayer under his breath and cuts into the child.

The operation is a success. Shon smiles and greets his parents with open arms, but they shrink away from him in horror. They cannot forgive what Franklin has done and take Shon away in the lamuda, the traveling robe for great journeys.

Out in Raider territory, Ivanova has no sooner tracked down one lone ship and blown it to smithereens than a fleet of them appear on her screen. When she comes back to base, the damage to her fighter suggests she was in a pretty big battle. "It was an educated risk," she says.

Franklin looks over some information on Shon's people. He stops short when he reads about the lamuda. He dashes out of medlab in sudden realization and runs *through Babylon 5, pushing people and aliens out of his way as he goes. He breaks into Shon's quarters, but it is too late. His parents are praying by his dead body, laid out on a ceremonial bed bathed in candlelight. "Oh my God," gasps Franklin. "You did it . . . You did it."*

"Do not grieve," says his mother. "This was not our son. This was only a shell." But Franklin cannot help himself. He staggers back against the wall and emotion overwhelms him.

Shon's death at the end of "Believers" shocked a lot of people. It is not the sort of thing that normally happens in· cozy television land. A TV episode is usually about presenting the main characters with a problem at the beginning, which they solve at the end. "Believers" doesn't do that. The characters wrestle with the problem throughout the episode, and each one comes to a solution that's right for him, but in the end this doesn't help Shon.

This sort of approach to storytelling is one that *Babylon 5* prides itself on, and the effect "Believers" had on the audience was planned from the outset. Joe Straczynski wrote a story premise that set down the basic dilemma, including a specific note about the ending, and gave it to David Gerrold to produce the script. "I didn't really want to do it at first," David admits. "I wasn't really thrilled with the story, which I thought had been done to death elsewhere. I said to him, 'Joe, why me?' He just said, 'Because you are the right one for it.' "

"I picked David for that because he had recently adopted a kid who was about the age of Shon," explains Joe Straczynski. "I always try to pair up the story with the writer, and I said, 'Halfway through the story you'll figure it out.' "

"Two or three weeks later and I'm midway through the scene where the parents are saying good-bye to their little boy," continues David Gerrold. "I had named him Shon, and my son's name is Sean, and midway through the scene tears are running down my cheeks. I realized *exactly* why Joe had given it to me."

"He called me in the middle of the night," Joe remembers,

"and said, 'You bastard! Now I understand why you wanted to give me this.' "

The resulting script was arguably the strongest one for Dr. Franklin in the first year, but at the time it was written, Richard Biggs hadn't been cast in the role. "They mailed the script of 'Believers' to me, and I thought, 'Oh my gosh, this is wonderful,' " says Rick. "I read it over and over again, and I thought, 'I've got to do this.' So I called my agent as they were hashing it out, and I said, 'Do whatever you have to do but get that contract signed!' "

The doctor's role on *Babylon 5* is very often to provide medical or technical information and serve the plot. Only when the plot concentrates on Franklin does he get the chance to shine. "Believers" not only gave him a chance to do that, it also established a firm foundation for the character. "It showed who the character was and what he believed in," says the actor. "This episode was 'Who is the guy behind the doctor? what does he believe? and what about religion? and how does he feel about death and dying? and what's the most important thing to him?—life.' "

"That was interesting, because I knew nothing about the character, nothing about the actor. I was essentially writing in a vacuum," adds David Gerrold. "I just invented this dilemma for him and invented the only way that it could be played, that a doctor can start thinking of himself as being God to his patients."

The episode is full of dilemmas for everyone. Franklin's dilemma, of course, is that he has the ability to save the child, even though the parents forbid him to do so. Sinclair's dilemma is that if he takes Franklin's side, the boy's life will be saved, but it will be at the cost of Babylon 5's neutrality. The parents' dilemma is that they must watch their son die, even though they love him very much. To David Gerrold, the portrayal of the parents was the key to getting the episode right. "When you think of parents refusing to give their child a life-saving operation, you don't think of them sympathetically," he says. "So that was the problem: that you come to the story already with your mind made up that the parents are not really terrific people."

He decided they had to be made sympathetic, because otherwise there would be no dilemma and the audience would automatically side with Franklin. So he showed them as sincere in their belief that a life-saving operation would actually kill the very essence of their son, and they refused the operation only because they loved him so much.

David Gerrold, like most of the freelance writers who contributed to the show, got the chance to go down to the set to see his episode being made. As fate would have it, one of the days when he wasn't on the set was the day when a problem arose over his script. "The actress playing the mother had a problem with a line of dialogue. She said, 'Can we get this rewritten? It's too poetic,' " he explains. "Joe said, 'You are going to have to play it the way it is written. The writer isn't available to rewrite it.' When I heard about that I was startled, because on any other show they would have said, 'Let's take a look at it,' but Joe just said, 'Play it as it's written,' which I think is an extraordinary vote of confidence in the writing. The actress went back to it and found a way to get into the line that allowed her to make it her own, and the challenge of getting in that way strengthened the performance. I would have been happy to adjust it for her, but essentially these people were very biblical in their own religion and there was a great deal of poetry and rhythm in their language, and I wanted it to be there."

In the midst of this is a subplot involving Ivanova's clash with a fleet of Raiders, which was slipped into the script by Joe Straczynski when the main plot came out a little short. It opens the episode out a bit by taking it into space and shows Ivanova's fighter-piloting skills but doesn't detract from the main thread of the story, which includes Michael O'Hare's favorite moment from the whole of the series.

Sinclair is faced with an impossible decision, torn between Dr. Franklin and the child's parents, who both believe what they are doing is right. Sinclair is the only one who asks what Shon wants. The boy's answer, of course, does nothing to make Sinclair's position any easier. He wants to live, but he doesn't want the operation. "That sums up a lot about Sinclair," says Michael. "I think the reason Sinclair is such a stickler for things to be done right, with honor and all that sort of thing, is because he really is a compassionate fellow. He has a dream or vision of his own that he really wants the station to work. And that little boy is really an example of the motivation for the mission because the idea is to make it safe for that little boy, so he can grow up and live his life and be a good fellow and hopefully do good things. It's very sad that later on his parents kill him because of their belief systems. Frankly, I have no sympathy for those parents."

The death of the boy is clearly what made the impact on most viewers in a world where television has trained its audience to expect a comfortable resolution at the end of an episode. The decision not to follow the TV formula is part of the *Babylon 5* philosophy. It is a future where problems still exist, where there are no easy answers, and where people make mistakes. It may be set in the future, but it mirrors the present. "As we were shooting 'Believers,' I was looking at a newspaper, and a couple in America were thrown in jail because they allowed their son to die rather than take him to a doctor because of their religious beliefs," recalls Rick Biggs. "I was thinking that the script correlates with things that are happening today, and I think that's why people connect to it so much. I think *Babylon 5* is showing that two hundred years from now people are going to be people and the problems that you see today are going to be problems of tomorrow."

"Everyone was right in that episode, and everyone was wrong in that episode," concludes Joe Straczynski. "I wanted to leave it where people would talk about it afterward. In that kind of situation, who is to blame? No one and everyone is the answer."

11
"Survivors"

Cast

Commander Jeffrey Sinclair ....Michael O'Hare
Lt. Commander Susan Ivanova ....Claudia Christian
Security Chief Michael Garibaldi ....Jerry Doyle
Ambassador Delenn ....Mira Furlan
Dr. Stephen Franklin ....Richard Biggs
Talia Winters ....Andrea Thompson
Vir Cotto ....Stephen Furst
Lennier ....Bill Mumy
Na'Toth ....Caitlin Brown
Ambassador G'Kar ....Andreas Katsulas
Ambassador Londo Mollari ....Peter Jurasik

Guest Stars

Lianna Kemmer ....Elaine Thomas
Cutter ....Tom Donaldson
Special Agent No. 1 ....David Austin Cook
Lou Welch ....David L. Crowley
ISN Reporter ....Maggie Egan
Nolan ....Jose Hosario
Young Lianna ....Robin Wake
Alien No. 1 ....Mark Hendriokoon
General Netter ....Rod Perry
Tech. No. 1 ....Marianne Robertson

An explosion rips apart one of the cobra bays, sending a maintenance technician, Nolan, tumbling out into space. He was lucky to survive. "If you call this survival,"
comments Dr. Franklin, as Nolan lies close to death in medlab.

It's a bad time for something like this to happen on Babylon 5. Earth president Santiago is about to visit the station to present a new fighter wing. Not surprisingly, when Major Lianna Kemmer of the president's security staff arrives on board, she demands to be briefed.

Something stirs inside Garibaldi as he hears her name. He was a friend of her father's seventeen years ago. "She was a real sweet kid," he remembers.

The sweetness that Lianna once had has trickled out of her, leaving a cold empty adult shell that oozes animosity as soon as Garibaldi walks into the room. She demands to take over the investigation, and he lets her without argument. The reaction is totally unlike him, and Sinclair knows it. The Michael Garibaldi he knew would never give up without a fight. Eventually, he corners Garibaldi and persuades him to talk.

Garibaldi had been working on Europa when the constant battle to uphold the law turned him to drink. It was then that he met Frank Kemmer and his daughter, Lianna. Garibaldi made a mistake, and Frank Kemmer got killed. He was blackballed throughout the system and sought comfort in alcohol. "Lianna," he says, "just died inside."

Now Lianna's injecting Nolan with a serum to get him to talk about the explosion, even though she knows it will kill him. In his last breath he names Garibaldi as the saboteur, something which is apparently confirmed by schematics of the cobra bay and a large quantity of Centauri ducats found in his quarters. Lianna orders him to be taken into custody, but Garibaldi kicks Security Officer Cutter and escapes. Suddenly, he is a wanted man on the run.

Wearing stolen clothes, he moves through the station, trying to find out who is framing him. Garibaldi eventually ends up alone in a bar with a bottle of booze. He pours himself a glass and stares at the inviting amber liquid as it catches the light. Then he downs it in one gulp. Before long he is drunk and stumbles out of the bar straight into Lianna's custody.

Fortunately for him, something interesting has turned up in Nolan's quarters, linking Nolan to the bomb and the pro-Earth group, the Homeguard. It seems he intended to sabotage President Santiago's visit, but the bomb went off as he was planting it. Garibaldi suspects that Lianna's assistant, Cutter, was involved and planted evidence in his quarters. But Cutter is wise to his suspicions and confronts him before he can find the second bomb.

It will be set off when the new fighter wing is launched, and as the countdown begins, Garibaldi and Cutter are in the middle of a fight. With each punch and kick, the countdown gets one step closer to zero. Somehow in the midst of this, Garibaldi grabs Cutter's link and screams into it, "Abort the drop!" Ivanova does so with only one second to spare.

Garibaldi knows he was lucky. He found himself repeating his old mistakes, crawling back into the bottle when things got too rough. "But you crawled back out again and did the job. That's what counts," Sinclair tells him. Even Lianna forgives him and thanks him for ensuring the success of President Santiago's visit. The president is fond of Babylon 5, she tells him, as they hug and say good-bye.

Garibaldi is a man with a tarnished reputation. He had been bounced from one station to another. His appointment to Babylon 5 was fiercely resisted, and he got the job at the insistence of Sinclair. This had been established as far back as "The Gathering," but we didn't find out why until "Survivors." It brought Garibaldi to the foreground for the first time, delved into his past, and showed that underneath this brash security chief was an insecure man who was frightened of being dragged back into alcoholism.

"It's something I knew a lot about, having seen it in several generations of my family," says Joe Straczynski, who handed over writing chores to Mark Scott Zicree for this one. "I wanted him [Garibaldi] to be someone who had a lot of hard times, been fired from almost every job he's ever had—and that's as good a reason as any to fire somebody. It gave him an internal scar and a constant threat by not drinking every day, and he could flip at any time and go back into it."

"I liked the story," says Jerry Doyle (Garibaldi). "To me, it had a lot of elements that as an individual in a story you like to see. It has a lot of different ways to go: you had humor, you had comedy, you had fighting, you get action and drama. There's no romance—there hasn't been much for my character anyway—but, yeah, it was a good story. I had the opportunity to work with some good people, and it was an enjoyable episode to shoot."

As the story opens, Garibaldi is a man who has learned to deal with his problem. He is seen constantly being in the presence of alcohol, repeatedly facing that temptation, and always refusing it. He sits down at the Zocalo bar with Sinclair and orders water. He is offered a drink by the well-meaning G'Kar and seeks help from Londo who, as usual, is nursing his own drink. The relationship between Londo and Garibaldi is an interesting and unusual one, made more so here because of the obvious parallels between their drinking habits. "What was wonderful for those two characters was they were loners," says Peter Jurasik, who plays Londo. "They had bitterness, they certainly had drinking in their past—or in their present in Londo's case—so they could relate to that. It was all polarization, but they became life rafts for each other to hold onto. It also pays off down the storyline when they lose each other.

"What's wonderful about Jerry Doyle is that on the set he really is the guy, along with Claudia [Christian, who plays Ivanova], who really keeps the set happy and light and reminds us of where we are, that we're making a television show," Peter continues. "I miss working with Jerry for that reason. He really is a very loose actor, maybe because he didn't come from as strong an acting background as some of us. He really uses it to his advantage. Whatever he may have lost with not having an education, he has gained in spades on the other sides. I really look back fondly—and I really mean that—on my work with Jerry."

It was only Jerry Doyle's second year in the acting business when he landed the role of Garibaldi. In his previous life he had been a commercial jet pilot, who then turned to the financial markets of Wall Street. When he switched to show business, he knew more about "business" than he did about "show" and wrote an almost entirely fictional résumé for himself to get an audition for *Babylon 5* (only giving the game away by claiming to have been part of the Harlem Dance Company—an all-*black* dance group!). "Survivors" gave him a chance to shine, and he certainly impressed director Jim Johnston. "It was a very good performance from Jerry. I think he's a better actor than they credit him, and he needs more roles like that that stretch him.

"Jerry and I worked a lot together," says Jim. "Jerry just tried to recall all those times when he had too much tequila or something, and we actually played scenes much longer than they were scripted. They all ended up in the picture because Jerry knew how to play that, just remembering from those tequila nights, and I think that's what made it."

The episode put Garibaldi through a lot of trials, as he is framed for sabotage and forced to go on the run. It was inevitable, perhaps, that he would fall back on old habits. "It was written that he ended up in the bar and he took a drink, and I didn't play it like that," says Jerry Doyle. "I played it that he always wanted to have a drink, and he ended up going to the place that he wanted to end up in, which is a bar. If you really wanted to be alone and by yourself, why would you go to a bar, where there's a lot of people and you know that they're going to be looking for you? So I thought that with all the things that were happening to him, with the things he was caused to remember, he wanted to have a drink."

It is not just one drink, of course: he gets blind drunk. "In the drunk scene in the bar, right before they yelled 'action,' I was standing up spinning in the direction opposite to the direction the director wanted me to go in," says Jerry. "So if you're spinning in a circle—you know what that feeling is— you don't have to be an actor to be dizzy, yet you have to know how much to spin and what direction to go in and that you can't fall out of frame. So that's a little trick to play to be inebriated."

Garibaldi staggers out of the bar into the clutches of Lianna. It was Jim Johnston's idea to bring in the little girl that he hallucinates as he looks up at Lianna and who says, "Drunk again, Uncle Mike?"

While Garibaldi's problems are being dealt with in the foreground of the episode, the background deals with the arrival of Earth president Santiago. The new fighter wing he presents to the station is important for forthcoming events, as is his high regard for Babylon 5. It makes his sub-sequent assassination in "Chrysalis" a double blow. But although the episode is all about the president's visit, he is never actually seen on the station. Joe Straczynski defends this on story grounds because the episode is really about the preparation for his arrival. The other reason why Santiago doesn't make an appearance is due to his fellow executive producer Douglas Netter.

"We couldn't see him [Santiago] because the picture we used of him was Doug, and Doug didn't want to do the role! We actually talked about a brief scene, showing him coming aboard and having Doug do it, but Doug vetoed that notion real fast," says Joe. "The plot sets up that there're different competing divisions within EarthForce over President Santiago. It sets up the first possible conspiracy against him. A lot of the first season is about laying threads that I pull into a knot in 'Chrysalis.' "

Despite obvious important developments in the arc, it is really the Garibaldi plot that makes the biggest impact. In typical TV fashion, he recovers from his addiction and makes up with Lianna, but because nothing is ever forgotten on *Babylon 5*, it is information that continues to inform the character throughout the series.

"He had all of the excuses he needed, and he fell off the wagon," concludes Jerry Doyle. "But I think it was about the dignity that anybody with a drinking problem must go through. If you fall off the wagon and [end up] drunk—you may have been sober for six years, eight years, two weeks, whatever your time frame is, whatever that struggle was—

people tend to want to pick on that one day. So I tried to play it as 'Yeah, I screwed up.' He fell off the wagon, but he got right back on and he walked out of there with a better knowledge and a strength and an understanding that he carries with him on to the next day, and the next day, and the next."

12
"By Any Means Necessary"

Cast

Commander Jeffrey Sinclair ....Michael O'Hare
Lt. Commander Susan Ivanova ....Claudia Christian
Security Chief Michael Garibaldi ....Jerry Doyle
Ambassador Delenn ....Mira Furlan
Dr. Stephen Franklin ....Richard Biggs
Talia Winters ....Andrea Thompson
Vir Cotto ....Stephen Furst
Lennier ....Bill Mumy
Na'Toth ....Caitlin Brown
Ambassador G'Kar ....Andreas Katsulas
Ambassador Londo Mollari ....Peter Jurasik

Guest Stars

Neeoma Connolly ....Katy Boyer
Orin Zento ....John Snyder
Senator Hidoshi ....Aki Aleong
Mary Ann Cramer ....Patricia Healy
Narn Captain ....Michael McKenzie
Eduardo Delvientos ....Jose Rey
Worker No. 2 ....Ricardo Martinez
Tech. No. 1 ....Marianne Robertson
Worker No. 1 ....Floyd Vaughn

The captain of the Tal'Quith is not happy. He has a valuable piece of cargo in his ship to deliver to Ambassador G'Kar, and the queue of vessels trying to dock at Babylon 5 is interminable. Ivanova appeals to Docking Supervisor Eduardo Delvientos to make room for the Narn ship, but the bays are hopelessly overcrowded. "Where the hell am I going to get the crew?" he protests. "We're already up to our butts out here!"

The Tal'Quith moves toward Bay 8, but sirens scream out a warning as the ship heads for a collision. In a panic, the captain disobeys orders from C&C and fires his engines, blowing out the cargo bay and ripping his ship apart. Rescue crews manage to fight through the flames and drag out the body of a dock worker. Delvientos rushes toward him. It is his brother, Alberto, and he is dead.

G'Kar knocks a glass off the table in rage, scattering shards around the room. The ship's cargo, a G'Quan Eth plant essential for the religious ceremony concluding the Holy Days of G'Quan, was destroyed in the accident. G'Kar must perform the ritual when the first rays of sunlight shine past the G'Quan mountains, but the only person on the station who has one of the flowers is Ambassador Londo Mollari—and he wants fifty thousand commercial credits for it.

"That's an outrage!" cries G'Kar.

"Of course, it's an outrage," says Londo with a victorious laugh.

Sinclair has found himself in the middle of an industrial dispute that is threatening to escalate into a crisis. The dock workers are angry at the way they are being treated and have gone on strike, even though it is forbidden in their contract. Their demands are clear. "You give us decent pay and equipment and hire enough workers to do the job safely, then we return to work."

The problem would be solved if only the Earth Senate would step in and give Babylon 5 the resources it originally promised. But the budget has been finalized, and they would rather send in negotiator Orin Zento to persuade the dockers to go back to work. Zento's speeches about how the government must cut costs make no impact on the workers, who are tired from working triple shifts with substandard equipment. So he invokes the Rush Act, empowering Sinclair to use any means necessary to get the dockers back to work.

Garibaldi leads his troops into the crowd of striking

dockers. Delvientos is ready for a fight and beckons them forward. Garibaldi puts them all under arrest, but Delvientos strikes out with his fist, punching Garibaldi across the jaw and causing the whole dock to erupt into a riot. Sinclair orders the troops to pull back, and the dockers raise their arms in victory as he faces the mob. With the full backing of the Rush Act, he claims the right to use "any means necessary" to end the strike and meets the dockers' demands by diverting money from Babylon 5's military budget.

Sinclair still has the dispute between G'Kar and Londo to settle and manages to persuade Londo to hand over the G'Quan Eth plant. This does nothing to pacify G'Kar, who has missed the appointed time for his religious ceremony. Sinclair reminds him, however, that sunlight takes time to travel in space and there are twelve hours before the sunlight that touched the G'Quan mountains ten years ago reaches the station. G'Kar thanks Sinclair heartily and, twelve hours later, conducts the ceremony in the Sanctuary in front of a backdrop of stars.

Kathryn Drennan had wanted to write for *Babylon 5* for a long time. As a working scriptwriter she had the qualifications to do so, but being the wife of the series' creator, J. Michael Straczynski, put her at a disadvantage. "I've always been very leery of nepotism," says Joe Straczynski. "It had to be something that no one else would have thought up for this show and no other science fiction show would do. When she came up with that notion [of the strike], I thought it was something worth pursuing because it's something we haven't seen a lot of. [But] because of my feelings about nepotism, I put a wringer on it, where she had to write the script up first and it had to go through all the gatekeepers: my story editor, Warner Bros. And it was the one we were hardest on for the entire season, because I thought we had to do that."

It became one of the more successful freelance contributions to the season, because of the way it focused on the behind-the-scenes realities of keeping a space station like Babylon 5 operational. By transplanting the industrial-relations problems of today into the twenty-third century, it plunged Sinclair into the middle of a dilemma that has resonances with the real world. That is one of the reasons why Michael O'Hare enjoyed the episode so much. "She writes very good dialogue," he says of Kathryn Drennan. "Joe is stronger in storytelling; she's very strong in dialogue—the relationship of character. I thought she had a very good gift for it, so I enjoyed doing it for that reason."

Sinclair looks progressively run-down throughout this episode. Small things like wearing his jacket undone and going unshaven contribute to conveying the obvious strain he is under. "I thought it was one of Michael's best performances," says the director, Jim Johnston. "It started because on the first day of shooting he'd just come in from New York—he had to go to New York at the weekend, where he's from—so he came back on the red-eye Monday morning, and he had to be taken right to the set and he looked like hell. I thought his performance was great that day; he wasn't so much acting, he was reacting, trying to get through the day. I said, 'Wait a minute, this is playing great.' So I didn't allow him to shave the rest of the week, and I said, 'Stay up late, I think you're best played tired,' and that's the way we pushed it."

The strike scenes actually feature an appearance by Jim Johnston, who stepped in front of the camera on the last day of shooting, not so much through ego but more through necessity. "I remember seeing newsreel footage of the Ford strikes and coal-mining strikes and people waving ball bats and shaking cars," he says. "Then there is that wonderful image when they all chant 'Strike, strike, strike.' I was going over my script and something was troubling me, and finally, I hit upon it: 'That's it, we keep talking about a strike, but we never actually go on strike.' I said, 'That's what we've got to do; we've got to cross that line and say strike.' I had this image of everybody saying, 'Strike, strike, strike,' so I called up John Copeland, the producer, told him my idea, and he said, 'Well, it's a great idea, but it's too late because the budget's already into Warners, and it's three thousand dollars to get a day player in and we can't open up the budget again.' I said, 'Okay, I understand.' But the next day I seethed and seethed, and when it came to the end of the day, I made the decision: 'Well, if they won't give me an actor, I'll give *them* an actor.' So I put one of those jumpsuits on, went into makeup, and said, 'Smear as much dirt on my face as possible,' then went to John Flinn, the cinematographer, and said, 'If I look silly, you'll never work in this town again!' and went out there and just did that line. Not only did I make it into the picture, but I was in the promo for the show!"

Others were also press-ganged into that scene to swell the number of extras. About twenty people in the crowd were actually members of the crew who were dragged in front of the camera by Jim Johnston.

While the strike is crippling the station, Londo and G'Kar are locked in a dispute over the G'Quan Eth plant. This continues to broaden the character of G'Kar, a process that began in "Mind War." "Now suddenly here's a religious side," says Andreas Katsulas, marveling at the way G'Kar has expanded from that very strident advocate of the Narn Regime seen in "Midnight on the Firing Line." "I just love this character. I don't think Bill Clinton, or whoever our ambassadors are in the United States, goes home and is spiritually active. And the plant is not just a token religion of 'Yes, I'm a Catholic' or 'Yes, I'm a Greek Orthodox,' or 'I'm a Baptist in name only and do the least amount possible.' Here's a character who lives his religion."

The discussion of Narn religion in "By Any Means Necessary" is indicative of the complexity of the alien cultures on Babylon 5. Not only do we get a glimpse of G'Kar as a follower of G'Quan, we also hear Na'Toth talk about her father as a Disciple of G'Lan, and these are two religious figures who will feature more prominently later on. As for Na'Toth, she isn't religious, preferring to believe in herself.

This is Julie Caitlin Brown's favorite moment from the episode.

"What I was developing—which, sad to say, never got played out because I didn't do the role anymore—was that originally her planet was run by women," says the actress. "Over the centuries the males took power. They were enslaved by the Centauri, and the women adapted to be warriorlike ... She was aware that all of these religious belief systems and all of these things that her people had clung to during their enslavement weren't getting the job done. So that's why she became a warrior. My dream was that she wanted to see it return to the power of the women and live peaceably, and that's why she says she believes in herself."

G'Kar's religious ceremony means nothing to Londo: he just sees it as an opportunity for revenge. Londo conspires to keep G'Kar from getting hold of the G'Quan Eth plant, and G'Kar retaliates by getting Na'Toth to steal one of the Centauri statues. It is a petty tit-for-tat squabble that reminds Peter Jurasik of schoolchildren. "There is a wonderful scene in that when they get yelled at in the Council Room," he says. "They sit like two little schoolboys—'I didn't do it; he made me do it.' It is a wonderful added facet to their characters. On one level it gives us that facet that 'Aren't these two people small-minded?' But it also gives us a bounce later on, like two schoolmates, when you finally grow up and you meet your little rival from the fifth grade who you used to fight with in grammar school, you realize, 'I like you; I'm glad I had you as a rival.' Although they continue to be rivals through the full series arc, a respect starts to happen over time, and pettiness like that is important to building that in."

It is, therefore, a very important episode in terms of the development of Londo and G'Kar. From the moment their rivalry is played out in "Midnight on the Firing Line," their lives are linked. Londo's prophetic dream that he will die with G'Kar's hands around his neck cements that relationship and "By Any Means Necessary" is another step along the road to that inevitable conclusion. "It is the very first episode in which we see Londo and G'Kar turning around in their respective orbits," says Joe Straczynski. "Before then it was always G'Kar baiting Londo, giving him a hard time, and here we see Londo being fairly mean and vile. This whole thing is out of spite, and for the first time, it is G'Kar who is being portrayed in a sympathetic fashion."

13
"Signs and Portents"

Cast

Commander Jeffrey Sinclair ....Michael O'Hare
Lt. Commander Susan Ivanova ....Claudia Christian
Security Chief Michael Garibaldi ....Jerry Doyle
Ambassador Delenn ....Mira Furlan
Dr. Stephen Franklin ....Richard Biggs
Talia Winters ....Andrea Thompson
Vir Cotto ....Stephen Furst
Lennier ....Bill Mumy
Na'Toth ....Caitlin Brown
Ambassador G'Kar ....Andreas Katsulas
Ambassador Londo Mollari ....Peter Jurasik

Guest Stars

Lord Kiro ....Gerrit Graham
Lady Ladira ....Fredi Olster
Raider No. 1 ....Whip Hubley
Dome Tech. No. 3 ....Anita Brabec
Kosh ....Ardwright Chamberlain
Dome Tech. No. 2 ....Joshua Cox
Man ....Garry Kluger
Fighter No. 1 ....Lee Mathis
Fighter No. 2 ....Douglas E. McCoy
Pilot ....Hector Mercado
Dome Tech. No. 1 ....Marianne Robertson
Reno ....Robert Silver
Morden ....Ed Wasser
Customs Guard ....Lynn Red Williams

*A fighter pilot is being chased by Raiders; he is fifty
percent down on power and hopelessly outnumbered.
He calls out to Babylon 5 for help, but the Raiders strike
with a final shot that destroys his starfury, sending
fragments flying into space. And he is just the latest
victim of the increasing number of Raider attacks.*

Meanwhile, a great long-lost Centauri treasure has been delivered to Londo. It is the Eye, an artifact so treasured by his people that he is breathless the first time he sees it. It will mean a great deal to the Centauri government, which is why Lord Kiro and Lady Ladira have arrived to collect it. But as soon as Ladira walks onto the station, she is overwhelmed by feelings of death and destruction and sees a frightening vision of Babylon 5 being engulfed in flames. Kiro takes little heed of her warning, just as he once dismissed her prophecy that he would be killed by Shadows.

There is another arrival on Babylon 5. He is Morden, a man in a smart suit with a pleasant smile that hides much mystery. He has come on a mission to ask each ambassador, "What do you want?" G'Kar wants to completely and utterly erase the Centauri. Londo wants to see a rebirth of glory and the Centauri commanding the stars. But when Morden meets Delenn, a wave of fatigue passes over her, a triangular symbol appears on her forehead, and she sees a dark shadow fall across his face. "They're here," she says.

Morden does not seek out the Vorlon ambassador but encounters him in the corridor as the Raiders' battle outside rocks the station. "Leave this place; they are not for you," says Kosh as the lights go out, and they are plunged into darkness. Later, Kosh asks for tools to repair his encounter suit, but he doesn't say why.

The leader of the Raiders pulls a gun on the Centauri delegation, shooting their aides dead and leaving Londo, Kiro, and Ladira exposed. "I want the Eye," he says, grabbing the precious object from Londo. He takes Kiro as a hostage and bundles him onto their ship.

"Very convincing performance," gloats Kiro, believing he has succeeded in his plot to take the Eye and seize power over the Centauri empire. But the Raiders were just using him as a tool. They want the Eye for themselves. Then a huge spidery vessel as dark as a shadow and covered in speckles of light appears out of nowhere. One blast from its weapons destroys the

*Raiders' ship, taking Kiro along with it and fulfilling
Ladira's prophecy.*

*With the Eye apparently gone for good, Londo fears
his career is over. And then Morden appears at his door
carrying a box. Londo opens it to find the Eye returned
to him in all its splendor. Morden tells him it is "from
friends you didn't know you had."*

*Sinclair also has friends he didn't know he had.
Garibaldi has been doing a little digging and found out
that the Minbari were the ones that insisted he be placed
in control of Babylon 5. Ladira tells him he may be in
control of a doomed station. With a touch to his
forehead, she shows Sinclair her vision of Babylon 5's
final moments as it explodes in a blaze of light. "This is
a possible future, Commander," she says, "and it is my
hope that you may yet avoid it."*

Signs and Portents," which gives its title to the season
as a whole, is one of the major episodes of the first
year. Most important, it introduces the Shadows and Morden's seemingly innocent question, "What do you want?"

"The show is built around two fundamental questions for
the first couple or three years," says Joe Straczynski. "The
first being 'Who are you?'; the second being 'What do you
want?'—on the theory that the answers to those questions
can either make you or they can destroy you, depending on
the order in which they are asked or answered. If you know
who you are before someone asks you what you want, the
answer will probably be fairly constructive. If you have not
gone through that process of self-examination and somebody asks you 'What do you want?', that answer might lead
you into a more destructive path. So those questions are
pivotal."

The agent of that question is Morden, as played by Ed
Wasser. "That was such a phenomenal way to come onto a
show," he says. "Such a great way to make an entrance,
because it was really mysterious—'What's up with that guy?
What does *he* want?' "

The audience's first impressions of Morden are colored by

a grandiose entrance as he walks confidently through an expansive corridor on the way to the Customs Area. "I really wanted to show that he was different to everyone else," says the director, Janet Greek. "Joe does a lot of very symbolic things. His name and everything is really very Arthurian, so we wanted that feeling of the outcast and somebody who never fits in. Not just an evil man; but an evil man who was all alone."

"Morden? Evil?" exclaims Ed Wasser. "No! It's obvious to you that Morden's very dark; there's a lot of evil energy behind Morden. Morden is self-righteous. He's amoral. He's not a bad guy: he just wants to be on the winning side. So Morden picks the side with all of the power, all of the strength."

His question, which he takes to every one of the alien ambassadors, gets to the heart of their characters. In the case of G'Kar, he is so consumed with his passion to destroy the Centauri that he hasn't given any consideration to what he might do if he achieved his desire. When Morden steps into the same room as Delenn, she senses Shadows (through the piece of the triluminary implanted into every member of the Grey Council) and orders him to leave. Kosh, it would seem, also senses Shadows, but we never get to see exactly what happens when the two characters meet in the darkened corridor. All we know is that Kosh's encounter suit is damaged.

"That scene was really weird," says Janet Greek. "Joe did not want it to be tangible: he wanted everyone to be puzzled and not quite know. And that's what happened. I would have liked to have revealed a little more and given the audience a little more, but Joe didn't want that, and when you work on that show you really are interpreting his vision."

The one person who gives Morden the right answer, of course, is Londo. "It is the centerpiece of where he sits," says the actor Peter Jurasik. "His heart and soul are stuck in a kind of muck that's bitter and bile and angry and unhappy with his position and place, both personally and politically. Londo is very much a political animal. He has a personal side and a political side, and both of those are stuck in the same bitter muck of 'My people didn't get what we deserve,' and it is a key moment to finally let it splatter all over the place. It is liberating for the character, too. That's what makes him the perfect person for Morden to align himself with."

"Signs and Portents" also brings in the idea of Babylon 5's impending destruction, later to be reiterated in "Babylon Squared" with Sinclair's flash-forward. The Centauri seer, Ladira, says it is only a potential future, yet it is one they are heading toward if they continue down their present path. It is one of the earliest examples of foreshadowing, a technique that Joe Straczynski has spread liberally throughout the story arc. "My feeling is there are a number of ways of creating tension," he says. "One is that you don't know what's going on. The Greek tragic mode, which you often see in Hitchcock movies, is where the audience knows something is going on, but the characters do not know necessarily. The process becomes 'How do you get there?' So throughout the series we'll often do this. We'll tell you flat out what's coming; we won't tell you how you get there, and with some things the 'there' is not what you think it is, or we may take you down a whole different road."

There was a great deal of discussion over how to portray Ladira's vision. Director Janet Greek remembers that the biggest concern was that it shouldn't go over the top. This was a problem that emerged as far back as auditioning actresses for the role. "Every single one of them, when they came in and went into a trance, went totally hysterical, and it really scared the producers," she says. "That was not what they wanted: they wanted it much more subtle. So when I actually did it, we decided a lighting change was not appropriate because it was just happening to her—it was her reality alone. So I toned it way down, and I don't think it was most effective that way. I should have gone for more spark and more fireworks and a bigger performance."

Like many of the most significant episodes of Babylon 5, "Signs and Portents" contrasts the drama with some of the most memorable light moments of the season. It begins with Ivanova being woken up early in the morning by her alarm and arriving in C&C still half asleep. When she tells Sinclair she hates getting up when it's dark outside, his obvious answer is "In space it's always dark."

"I actually thought about it a lot," says Claudia Christian, who plays Ivanova. "It adds a whole new element to your character when you realize you have been living in a space station and you have never been outside and you have never seen or breathed fresh air or just taken a walk down a street. Me, myself, personally, I'd get claustrophobia. I'd go crazy! I'd be running up and down Grey Sector; I'd probably know every inch of the station because of my inability to stay in one place at one time . . . I think you get a little stir-crazy once in a while. I think that's why she likes to go out and fight in the starfuries. It's her way of going outside for a while."

The other memorable moment is Londo and G'Kar's argument while waiting for the transport tube with a poor unfortunate Human stuck in the middle. "We had such a good time doing that together," says Peter Jurasik. "It was a scene that started to bond Andreas and I as two actors, because the scene took a great deal of trust for us to do. We had to really rehearse it and work it together. It simultaneously made me respect Andreas as an actor and also realize what a wonderful complement we could be. So it was an important scene in that sense, for the development, not only of Andreas and Peter, but for G'Kar and Londo, too."

As far as the story arc is concerned, the most important moment comes toward the end of the episode. When the dark spidery ship comes out of nowhere and destroys the Raiders, it is the audience's first glimpse of a Shadow vessel. The significance of this moment is obvious only in hindsight, and this was a deliberate move by Joe Straczynski. "The best part of that was knowing from the reaction of the fans when the Shadow vessel came out of nowhere and blasted it [the Raider ship] to hell that they were knocked down by it thinking 'What on Earth is this?' A lot of folks didn't really see that it meant anything; it just came out of the blue. But it was a very important process of setting up the later points of the arc."

14
"TKO"

Cast

Commander Jeffrey Sinclair ....Michael O'Hare
Lt. Commander Susan Ivanova ....Claudia Christian
Security Chief Michael Garibaldi ....Jerry Doyle
Ambassador Delenn ....Mira Furlan
Dr. Stephen Franklin ....Richard Biggs
Talia Winters ....Andrea Thompson
Vir Cotto ....Stephen Furst
Lennier ....Bill Mumy
Na'Toth ....Caitlin Brown
Ambassador G'Kar ....Andreas Katsulas
Ambassador Londo Mollari ....Peter Jurasik

Guest Stars

Walker Smith ....Greg McKinney
The Muta-Do ....Soon-Teck Oh
Caliban ....Don Stroud
Rabbi Koslov ....Theodore Bikel
Gyor ....James Jude Courtney
Andrei Ivanov ....Robert Phalen
ISN Reporter ....Lenore Kasdorf
Migo ....Michael McKenzie
Tech. No. 1 ....Marianne Robertson

Garibaldi rips a medlab package from two illicit dealers in the Zocalo, sending the Earther tumbling into one of the sales carts and dispensing the alien with a punch. He turns his back on them as he links in with security and doesn't see the Earther pull a makeshift knife from his clothes and lunge forward. A beefy punch stops the Earther microseconds before the blade plunges into Garibaldi's back. Garibaldi turns and smiles when he sees the man who punched his attacker. It's Walker Smith, an old friend.

Smith was a prizefighter with a shot at the title until he got framed for taking drugs. Now he wants to make a splash by becoming the first Human to fight in the Mutai, the trial of blood. "Are you out of your skull?" says Garibaldi. But Smith is deadly serious.

The door to Ivanova's quarters opens, and she stares open-mouthed at her visitor. It is Rabbi Koslov, who has come to see her about the death of her father. He is taken aback when she tells him her duties haven't permitted her to sit shivah, so he asks Sinclair if she can have some time off. Ivanova is furious. "My father always tried to control my life when he was alive," she says with tears in her eyes. "I don't need anyone to take his place now that he's gone."

Smith and Garibaldi watch Gyor, the master of the Mutai, slug it out in the ring with a Drazi, kicking him and punching him relentlessly until the Drazi is knocked helpless to the floor. The Muta-Do turns to the crowd and asks if anyone is brave enough to challenge Gyor. "I am," declares Walker Smith. Garibaldi looks at him horrified.

Gyor attacks Smith in the ring with a fierceness born of confidence, striking him with a punch, a kick, a head-butt. Smith picks himself up off the floor and fights back viciously, giving back punches and kicks of his own that send Gyor stumbling backward. They are both bloody and unsteady on their feet, but they keep going, exchanging punches that send each other reeling but don't stop them from coming back for more. Two final punches, and they both fall to their knees. The fight is declared a draw. The crowd chants for their champion, "Gyor! Gyor! Gyor!" but Gyor puts up a hand to silence them and lead them in a new chant, "Smith! Smith! Smith!"

Ivanova watches Rabbi Koslov as he stands in the queue of people waiting for their transport back to Earth. And as she does so, her mind drifts back to her father's last words: "A father should give his daughter love as well as respect, and in that I failed you . . .

Forgive me." Something stirs in her, and she runs up to the rabbi. "Stay," she tells him. "Help me sit shivah."

Ivanova, dressed in black, listens to Rabbi Koslov talk about her father, a man who was devoted to peace. She also reminisces, smiling and laughing about times from her childhood. She thanks everyone who is gathered with her to share her time of sorrow. "You have helped me to find someone long lost and very precious to me," she says. "The father I loved." She takes the Jewish prayer book and recites the Mourning Prayer. As she says "Amen," all the grief that had been bottled up inside her since her father died comes out, and she cries openly, taking comfort on Sinclair's shoulder.

The two separate stories in "TKO" came from two equally separate sources. The boxing plot came from the story editor, Lawrence G DiTillio, who wanted to introduce some kind of sport onto Babylon 5. Football was clearly impractical for a space station, so his mind turned to boxing. "It just involved two men in a ring. There is an audience, but by cheating shots you could make ten or twenty people look like several hundred people," he says. "I thought about it and went in and pitched it, and they said, 'Nah, nah, we can't do it, no way.' I said, 'Okay,' and I went away to look for something else. In the interim, I mentioned it to Jim Johnston, who I worked with a lot as a director, and Jim got hot-bothered! He just got totally wild. He said, 'I know how to do it. It's great. We can do it within the budget. It's terrific!' He went into Doug [Netter, the executive producer] and threw such a pitch at Doug that he said, 'Okay, this is going to be a great story, and Jim is going to do it.' "

When it came time to film the episode, however, Jim Johnston wasn't able to do it. It was scheduled to follow directly after "Babylon Squared," and there was no way he could direct that show and at the same time prepare for "TKO." So the directing chores passed to John C. Flinn III. Not that it was much of a chore, because John Flinn had always wanted to direct *Babylon 5*, ever since he joined the show as director of photography. His previous directing credits came from *Magnum, P.I.* and *Jake and the Fatman*, so he found *Babylon* 5 a little different. "I've always done the cowboys and Indians and the cops and robbers," he says. "The next thing I know I'm in space, and it's a whole different world there. It's *really* a different world."

"TKO" was a good place for him to start because he loves action. "I talked to Greg McKinney, who played Walker Smith, and I said, 'Doubles are great, but in this deal, I need somebody who is really in shape.' I said, 'I need you to act in all these scenes, I need you to fight, can you do this? Can you do that?' He assured me that he was in shape, and he showed me some things and proved to me that he could handle it—and did he ever! When I want action, I want *action*, and I want faces in the camera, and I want to see that I've got my real guys there. I was very fortunate to have great stunt guys who could act, too. James Jude Courtney [as Gyor] was excellent. These guys with all the makeup they had on on the Mutai side, they didn't break a sweat, and I kept them going for hours and hours. I was so fortunate that everybody was physically fit to do this part. It wasn't easy."

The boxing plot changed considerably from what was originally planned. Larry DiTillio wrote the script intending the fight to be more savage and alien. "I happen to be a sumo fan," he says. "I know it's very strange, I'm not Japanese, but I'm a big sumo fan, and I wanted something that had people really beating each other to death but not doing it out of anger, doing it as a sport and with a sense of honor. I also wanted an older character for the main guy [Smith]. My original concept was that this was a character that was not a budding champion but was kind of like an old tug who had actually thrown fights and was doing a lot of tank fights and wanted one last shot at becoming a champion . . . My original theory was to have the guy beaten to death, but that he had gotten some redemption by taking his shot. It didn't work out that way because we went with younger casting, and Joe felt that it was a little too depressing."

"I thought the kick-boxing part was not as special as it could have been," adds Joe Straczynski. "What was exceptional about it, of course, is the 'sitting shivah' part of the episode, which is commendable because we have not seen much of other cultures in the future in space. Everyone seems to be either British or American. There isn't much in the way of Jews or Muslims or anything of a non-Western point of view, and so it was important to show that these people do go on in our cultures, whatever they happen to be, and our heritage continues."

The seed of the idea came from "Born to the Purple," in which Ivanova's father used the last moments of his life to tell her all the things he wanted to tell her. But she never really got the chance to air her feelings in return. This had been weighing on Larry DiTillio's mind for much of the season, until Joe Straczynski told him that Ivanova is Jewish. "I said, 'Here we have the perfect setup, because in the Jewish religion you sit shivah for the dead,'" Larry remembers. "At the same time, I thought, it's interesting to think about what would happen to certain religions if, in fact, we did discover aliens out there . . . Originally, I set out to do a show which had Ivanova thinking about her Jewishness. Was she a Jew? Did she believe what she had been taught as a child? Which is a nice area, but it's much more philosophical than it is dramatic."

By allowing Ivanova to reexamine her feelings about her father, it afforded her a great deal of emotion. First of all, we see the more familiar Ivanova, the military officer with no time for personal trivia. Then she begins to crack, and we see the Ivanova who has been lurking underneath, the Ivanova who hasn't been able to grieve for her father. "It was a great episode for me," says the actress Claudia Christian. "It gave me a chance to do a little bit of acting and explain a little bit more about my character. Theodore Bikel [Rabbi Koslov] was really fun to work with. He had so many stories and so many great old memories and a lot of jokes, so we kept laughing with the whole thing.

"I liked when I was telling the story," she adds. "It seemed like it was a healing process to be talking about it, and you really hadn't seen her be that relaxed and comfortable before. It was a more familial feel than the way she is at work, and it seemed it was a little more natural than a lot of the dialogue that I [have]. I mean, the dialogue is obviously incredible—it's just that sometimes, with the technobabble, you tend to sound a little stilted whether you like it or not. Talking about tachyon emissions isn't the same as talking about when you were five and your father saved you from embarrassment."

They were very emotional scenes, from the joy of remembering the good times with her father to the moment she lets out her grief by crying. "To this day I have been with her, just walking, and somebody's stopping her and saying they love what she did when she sat shivah," says John Flinn. "I think they are the best moments she has done on this series. She is such a good actress. She had everybody sitting there in tears."

Claudia returns the compliment to her director. As a former actor himself, he has experienced being on that side of the camera. "He's very sensitive, and he's good with the actors," she says. "He takes a lot of time to work with you, and a lot of directors that come in just worry about the CGI [computer-generated imaging] and how's it going to look and 'let me get the biggest crane and the biggest shot and the most extras,' and they forget about us. They assume, 'Well, you're doing fine.' Sometimes you don't want to just do fine, you want to do well."

The episode split the fans between those who prefer the boxing plot and those who prefer the Ivanova side of the story, but it is the sitting shivah plot that won over the most people. It even came to the notice of a Jewish organization that monitors television and film and earned Babylon 5 the first of its many awards.

15
"Grail"

Cast

Commander Jeffrey Sinclair ....Michael O'Hare
Lt. Commander Susan Ivanova ....Claudia Christian
Security Chief Michael Garibaldi ....Jerry Doyle
Ambassador Delenn ....Mira Furlan
Dr. Stephen Franklin ....Richard Biggs
Talia Winters ....Andrea Thompson
Vir Cotto ....Stephen Furst
Lennier ....Bill Mumy
Na'Toth ....Caitlin Brown
Ambassador G'Kar ....Andreas Katsulas
Ambassador Londo Mollari ....Peter Jurasik

Guest Stars

Aldous Gajic ....,,.David Warner
Deuce ....William Sanderson
Jinxo ....Tom Booker
Ombuds Wellingston ....Jim Norton
Mirriam Runningdear .... ,,,......Linda Lodge
Kosh ....Ardwright Chamberlain
Mr. Flinn .... ,,,....................John Flinn
Tech. No. 1 ....Marianne Robertson

*Mirriam Runningdear screams in fear as an alien
tentacle reaches out toward her. She is shackled to a
chair, unable to move. Deuce, a crime boss from Down-
Below, watches as the tentacle latches onto her forehead
and sucks out every thought she ever had. Then it
slithers back inside a Vorlon encounter suit. Deuce turns
to the petrified man beside him, a loser nicknamed
Jinxo, and warns him to pay up on his debts or get fed
to "Ambassador Kosh."*

*Aldous Gajic has arrived on Babylon 5 in his quest to
find the Holy Grail. He is not on the station for more
than a few minutes before Jinxo steals his credit chips.*

*Garibaldi grabs Jinxo and hauls him up before the
Ombuds, who is bewildered to discover Thomas
"Jinxo" Jordan has enough qualifications to land himself
a good job in a dozen other places. The Ombuds offers
to help by giving him free passage off Babylon 5. "You
can't do that!" cries Jinxo from the dock. "I've got to
stay here!"*

*Aldous offers to take Jinxo under his wing, and Jinxo
explains he can't leave the station because he has the
Babylon curse. He worked on constructing the other
four stations, and each time he left one, it was sabotaged
or blew up or disappeared. He believes if he leaves
Babylon 5, it will also be destroyed.*

*Dr. Franklin finds that Mirriam Runningdear's wiped
brain bears all the hallmarks of a Na'ka'leen feeder, an
animal kept under heavy quarantine in the Centauri
sector. This means Deuce was using a replica of Kosh's
encounter suit to make people believe the Vorlons were
working for him.*

*Meanwhile, Deuce's thugs are out looking for Jinxo.
As soon as they spot him, Jinxo makes a run for it,
leaving Aldous to stand his ground. He raises his staff,
knocking one of them to the floor, but the other one hits
him with a shock stick and he collapses, unconscious.
When Aldous wakes up, he is facing the feeder, along
with the kidnapped Ombuds. Aldous talks to it softly,
urging it out into the open. Inexplicably, it obeys. Its
three snakelike tentacles emerge from the fake Vorlon
encounter suit and carry it into the middle of the room.*

*They all turn as Garibaldi's men burst in with Sinclair
and Jinxo in tow. Deuce's people scatter, and the feeder
jumps up to the ceiling. Jinxo tries to undo the
Ombuds's bonds as the security team nervously watches
the feeder. Deuce takes his opportunity, steps out from
his hiding place, and aims his PPG at Jinxo. Aldous
jumps in to protect him and takes Deuce's gun blast in
the arm. He collapses to the floor and is left helpless as
the feeder approaches them. The members of the security
team aim their weapons and fire in a concentrated burst,*

*splattering the feeder's body all over the walls and floor.
But it is all too late for Aldous; he knows he is dying.
"My search is over," he says. "I've failed . . . No one
left . . ." Jinxo vows to take over his search, and Sinclair
bears witness to the act. Then, in his last moments, a
calmness falls over Aldous, and he smiles up at Jinxo. "I
see it, Thomas," he says. "The Grail . . ."*

*No one believes in Jinxo's Babylon curse, but
nevertheless, Sinclair, Ivanova, and Garibaldi gather in
the Observation Dome to watch him leave. The
jumpgate swallows him up, they wait, but there is no
"boom." "No boom today," Ivanova corrects them.
"There's always a boom tomorrow."*

If there was one moment from the first season that got
everyone chuckling, it was the scene in "Grail" where a
man tries to sue an alien because its grandfather allegedly
abducted his grandfather. "It always struck me as being a
funny notion," says Joe Straczynski, who dropped the scene
into Christy Marx's script. "We've had these tales of abduc-
tion going on now for quite some time, and if we did make
contact with aliens and they were doing this, it is going to
come into someone's mind 'Sue 'em!' It seems a very logical
way to go. Somebody is going to try to do this at some
point—this is actually going to happen!—so it was a fine
notion. I mentioned it to Christy and said, 'I want to put this
into your script,' and she had no problem with that."

The scene even has a little in-joke for the crew, because
the man who plays Mr. Flinn is in fact John C. Flinn III, far
better known for his work behind the camera as *Babylon 5*'s
director of photography. "It was so funny," he says. "I'm
reading the script, and I see this 'Well, Mr. Flinn . . .' and I
go, 'Well, that's funny. Joe's even spelled it the right way.' "

John Flinn was an actor before he switched careers but
didn't realize what Joe Straczynski was planning for him
until it was too late. "I walk in the office and say 'Joe, who's
doing this guy Flinn?' and he goes, 'You are.' I said, 'Joe, no,
I've got two pages of dialogue here. It's been twenty years
since I've acted. Maybe we better have a reading.' He said,

'Learn your lines.' I was stuck because it got out immediately, so everybody knows I'm doing it. I can't back out; there's no way. He chose me. I've got to do it, right? So I did it, and the crew was so great to me. They had a chair with coffee and doughnuts and this whole thing for me. They did the whole trip. I admit, I was a little bit nervous because I haven't done it in so long. It was fun, but I was sure glad when it was over!"

The focus of the episode is the search for the Holy Grail. Once again, it brings out the mystical theme that is often explored in *Babylon 5*, going back to the discussion about souls in "Soul Hunter" and continuing through the religious references, particularly in the case of the Minbari. "The Grail has a very mythic element to it," says Joe. "Christy brought in the Cup of the Goddess and mentioned that this isn't just a Christian legend—it does have its roots further into history than that. And there is some nice character stuff with David Warner."

David Warner, who played Aldous Gajic, brought a sense of majesty to the part. As Lennier says, "He has the look." His serenity comes from the purpose that his search has given him, even though that search may never be concluded in his lifetime. In many ways, the episode tells his story, from the moment his family was killed and he lost faith in his job as an accountant, to the moment that the numbers started to add up again when he took on the mission to find the Grail, and to the moment when he finds what he was looking for. Whether or not what he sees when he dies is really the Grail and whether or not he finds regeneration and salvation in the afterlife is not really important. What is important, as Delenn remarks, is that he believes he found everything he was looking for.

"He's a wonderful actor. He was wonderful to work with," says Michael O'Hare. "They make a mistake. They often cast him as sinister. Sometimes it happens with the Brits— they get cast as sinister because of the eloquence and the expression they often have and the intellect they often have. It makes 'sinister' exciting. We should change that. This fellow in particular they should cast in more warm roles."

In Aldous we see a man who had a purpose to his life and achieved his goal. In Jinxo we see a man who has changed his life by finding a new purpose. And in Sinclair we see a man who is still searching for a purpose. When Sinclair comments that it is hard to spend your life searching for something and never finding it, he is really talking about himself. "I think most people in a leadership position—if they've got any decency to them at all—are looking for some kind of ennobling, unifying concept to give them something to inspire them," says Michael. "Will is born of inspiration, and the heart is the conduit to the mind. So if you're in that position, you're looking for something you can hold on to, which is why you put up with so much self-sacrifice."

The theme also reflects on the other characters on Babylon 5. Most of the Humans consider Aldous's search a complete waste of time, while the Minbari see his mission as a noble and honorable one. Londo sees it as an opportunity to make some money in return for doing a little research, while Vir is so keen to be helpful that he does the research in advance. "I think he was kind of neurotic and worried about everything. He just wanted everything to be right," says Stephen Furst in defense of his character. "He was a people-pleaser. He wanted to do his best."

Other character moments picked out by "Grail" center on Garibaldi's primitive eating habits. At the beginning of the episode he is seen wolfing down his meal. This has been repeated on several occasions, going right back to "Midnight on the Firing Line" when Ivanova comments, "Garibaldi, you eat like a starving man." By the time we get to "Grail," it becomes clear that something is going on with Garibaldi and food.

"When we got going in the series itself," Jerry Doyle explains, "the writers, Joe, Larry DiTillio, and a couple of the other people sat down with us, asked us about our likes, dislikes, passions, fears, hobbies, interests, family background, education, and all of that stuff. I think they tried to incorporate a lot of those elements into the character. My character likes to cook, which I do in life. I don't eat the way the character eats, but I think in the pace of the show with the things that we're doing and the elements that we're up against, you don't have time to have a leisurely meal. You usually stuff it down, get on to the next thing, and hopefully it stays down. It's especially bad after lunch. You have a big lunch, and they say, 'Okay, now we're going to do scene so-and-so,' and you go, 'Oh God, I have to eat that chicken!' Then something screws up, and you have to do it again and again and again, and it's just like 'Oh man!' "

The other side of the episode concerns the Na'ka'leen feeder, which provides the jeopardy and action for the story, contrasting with the more philosophical aspects raised by Aldous's search for the Holy Grail. It reiterates the mystery over the true nature of the Vorlons and what really lies beneath their encounter suits. Kosh's response when Sinclair points out that his encounter suit makes people nervous about what is inside is typical. "Good," he says.

There were behind-the-scenes problems with "Grail" that tend to color the episode for Joe Straczynski. There was a disagreement over the way it was directed, and it became Richard Compton's final outing on *Babylon 5*, both as a director and as a coproducer. What saves the show, in Joe's mind, is the Na'ka'leen feeder, which was entirely created using CGI. "That is the first time, for sure, that a computer-graphics creature of that complexity had ever been done for television," he says. "That had about seventy percent [of the] resolution of the *Jurassic Park* dinosaurs. That showed us the outer window of what we could do with our effects. That one took almost two weeks of rendering time, so we realized, 'Okay, we can do this, but we could only do it once a season.' "

16
"Eyes"

Cast

Commander Jeffrey Sinclair ....Michael O'Hare
Lt. Commander Susan Ivanova ....Claudia Christian
Security Chief Michael Garibaldi ....Jerry Doyle
Ambassador Delenn ....Mira Furlan
Dr. Stephen Franklin ....Richard Biggs
Talia Winters ....Andrea Thompson
Vir Cotto ....Stephen Furst
Lennier ....Bill Mumy
Na'Toth ....Caitlin Brown
Ambassador G'Kar ....Andreas Katsulas
Ambassador Londo Mollari ....Peter Jurasik

Guest Stars

Colonel Ari Ben Zayn ....Gregory Martin
Harriman Gray ....Jeffrey Combs
Tragedy ....Macaulay Bruton
Sofie Ivanov ....Marie Chambers
Lou Welch ....David L. Crowley
General Miller ....Frank Farmer
Comedy ....Drew Letchworth
Tech. No. 1 ....Marianne Robertson

"What sort of machine is this?" Lennier asks, staring at the thing taking up most of Garibaldi's quarters. It's a motorcycle, or, at least, it will be as soon as he can figure out how to put it together. Lennier's eyes light up when Garibaldi tells him it is a piece of Earth history. "History?" he says. "That is an interest of mine." And he offers his assistance.

Colonel Ari Ben Zayn faces Sinclair across the briefing table, his Psi Corps assistant, Harriman Gray, at his side. They're "Eyes," internal investigators, on a mission to check the loyalty of Babylon 5's command staff and are armed with new regulations to make

*everyone submit to a telepathic scan. Ivanova refuses to
cooperate, and Sinclair promises he won't let
it happen.*

*But that night Ivanova sees herself walking down the
Central Corridor in the misty half world of dreams.
Through the mist she sees her mother, flanked by two
men from Psi Corps, their faces hidden by comedy and
tragedy masks. "Mamma?" she screams, as Tragedy
holds an injection to her mother's arm. "Only one way
out," her mother assures her as drugs are shot into her
system. Ivanova looks back to see that her mother's face
has changed into her own, echoing her mother's words.
"Only one way out . . ."*

*Ivanova wakes up with a scream. Minutes later she is
in Sinclair's quarters handing in her resignation. He
refuses to accept it. "You're too important to me," he
tells her. "Besides, I've found a way to avoid the scans."*

*EarthForce law states that telepathic scans can be
used only to check the truth of specific charges. So when
Ben Zayn "interviews" Sinclair, he is forced to do so
without Gray. He questions every decision of his
command: Ragesh 3, Deathwalker, the dockers'
strike . . . Then Ben Zayn plays his trump card,
accuses Sinclair of working against the interests of
EarthForce, relieves him of command, and takes
control of Babylon 5 for himself.*

*Sinclair is wading through records on EarthForce law
when Garibaldi interrupts him. He's been doing a little
bit of digging of his own and found that Ben Zayn
was one of the people passed over for command of
Babylon 5 and is a friend of Bester, the Psi Cop.*

*When Sinclair goes back into the interrogation room,
facing Gray this time as well as Ben Zayn, he asks the
telepath, "Will you be scanning the colonel as well?"
With that seed planted in Harriman Gray's thoughts,
Sinclair turns the tables on Ben Zayn and becomes the
interrogator. "It must have stuck in your craw when you
were passed over for command of Babylon 5," he says.*

"There was nothing you could do, of course, until your friend Bester thought of a way to get even."

The bitter truth provokes anger in Ben Zayn, and Gray senses it. *"I can feel the hatred in you,"* he says. *"It's sick, deep, filthy."* Ben Zayn strikes Gray across the face and knocks him to the floor. He pulls a gun on Sinclair and circles around the table. *"Colonel,"* says Gray. *"Pain!"* Ben Zayn tenses as pain stabs through his mind. In that moment of distraction, Sinclair throws a punch and decks Ben Zayn, concluding the investigation.

Garibaldi returns to his quarters astonished to discover Lennier has finished rebuilding his motorcycle. They wheel it out and ride it down the Central Corridor, whooping with delight. *"It's good to have things back to normal,"* Ivanova comments, as Garibaldi and Lennier zoom off into the distance.

"Eyes" was a last-minute addition to *Babylon 5*'s first season, which had to be written when a freelance writer fell through on delivering a script. Joe Straczynski was at home with the flu working on "Voices of Authority," which left the story editor, Larry DiTillio, with the job of coming up with something, and coming up with it quickly. "The parameters were: 'Okay, Larry, come up with a story that can be done in two rooms, that has no spaceships, no special effects, no CGI, no makeups, and is really about three characters sitting in a room. And, by the way, write it in five days so we can prep it.' I thought, 'Oh, great!' "

He used it to reexamine all of the controversial decisions Sinclair had made over the course of the season, from the Ragesh 3 incident to the destruction of Deathwalker through to the dockers' strike. On each occasion Sinclair either directly went against orders from Earth or bent the rules to suit his own agenda. "Because he was trying to do the right thing," says Michael O'Hare (Sinclair). "There're always enemies when you're in a position of power, and they'll use anything you've done, even the good things, to get back at you. But they failed, and as Sinclair showed in that episode, he's quite capable of being extraordinarily fierce, rather like an English bulldog, if it's necessary. And the fellow who went after him ended up in pretty bad shape for his trouble."

It also takes the opportunity to expand the telepathy theme, showing an ordinary member of the Psi Corps as sympathetic. This character, who became Mr. Gray, was originally written as a midget woman who was accepted into the Psi Corps after facing discrimination outside because of her height. Some small people were even brought in to read for the part before it was decided to go with more conventional casting. The script was rewritten to include Gray's military background, which allowed him to have a position within the organization as a military specialist.

The episode also expands Ivanova's hatred of the Psi Corps and her fear of being scanned. It is something that manifests itself in the dream in which Ivanova sees herself being put into the same position as her mother had been. "I used a lot of smoke in that scene," says the director, Jim Johnston. "I also shot it a little bit off-speed. Instead of all twenty-four frames [per second], I shot it at off-speeds of twenty-two, twenty-three. It would probably take a cinematographer to know it, but you look at the movement of the people, and it's off, like a dream sequence should be. I don't think a dream sequence should be this beautiful flowing misty thing, because I think dreams come to you in spurts, and I tried to make that happen with the camera to take it out of reality. Claudia did a great job, too. It's difficult to bring all those emotions up in a scene like that."

"I loved that actress who played my mother," says Claudia Christian. "She was wonderful. She was a very good actress, and she had a very interesting look. I thought we definitely looked like we could be related. It was cool. I like those dream sequences."

Ivanova's fear of being scanned comes to a head in "Eyes," when it becomes increasingly clear that she will either have to submit to a scan or be charged with insubordination. It brings the pent-up emotions of this very militaristic officer bubbling to the surface. "There must be twenty episodes where I just get to the verge of tears," says Claudia. "They don't want Ivanova—and I don't want her—to cry too much, so I try to tear up emotionally and then suck it back in. I happen to be quite talented at the art of almost crying."

Her frustration eventually spills over in the bar when a drunk makes a move on her that, in retrospect, he probably wishes he hadn't. Ivanova lashes out and ends up trashing the bar and most of its clientele. It was a rare chance for Ivanova to get involved in the action and for Claudia Christian to demonstrate her fighting skills. "We were rehearsing the fight while everyone else was off shooting another scene, and Kerry [Rossall], the stunt coordinator, was showing me the moves," she says. "He wanted me to bash someone's head into the bar, and he used his own head as an example. There was this black cloth on the bar, and underneath it, unbeknownst to him, was a metal art object. He bashed his head on the bar, and he hit this metal object really hard, so he was bleeding and he had a big lump and it was quite dramatic. It kind of put a big spin on the fight scene when I was doing that. I kept thinking of poor Kerry with the big egg on his head!"

The drama of the episode contrasted with the story of Garibaldi's motorcycle and Lennier's miraculous attempts at rebuilding it. The motorbike in question was a Kawasaki, which made its way aboard the space station courtesy of the Kawasaki company, which had agreed to sponsor the show. "I said, 'If I have to do a product placement, at least let me make a story out of it,' " remembers Larry DiTillio. "I thought this was kinda cool, and I thought it was kinda funny. But we fought throughout the production. I said, 'You can't have him build this motorcycle and not show the two of them on it riding down the corridors of Babylon 5.' And they said, 'No, no, no, it's dangerous.' I was going to have them crashing, and they said, 'No, no, no,' but Jim said, 'Oh yeah, we have to have them ride the motorcycle.' So eventually, they realized that they had to ride the motorcycle, and Ivanova and Sinclair's reaction is pretty priceless as they go by."

As director, Jim Johnston also wanted to dress Garibaldi in Marlon Brando–style leathers for that final shot, but he lost the battle and Garibaldi and Lennier rode through the Central Corridor in their ordinary costumes. The shot had to be created inside the computer because *Babylon 5*'s insurance company wouldn't allow two valuable actors to go speeding through an expensive set on a 1052cc bike. Perhaps it was just as well, because Jerry Doyle, who plays Garibaldi, has no love for the machines. "Scared to death of them," he says. "I rode a Triumph 650 once. I got to the corner, and I was going way too fast and didn't know how to stop it, so I ended up laying it down and sliding it across the road into somebody's lawn!"

The motorbike scenes include one where Lennier is performing a chant over the machinery. This got the actor, Bill Mumy, into a lot of trouble when he decided that an appropriate chant would be the title of the latest album by his band, the Jenerators. "I believe I was chanting Zabagabee, which is the name of our 'Greatest Hits,' " he says. "It was unbelievable to me that Joe Straczynski, who was watching the dailies [rushes], comes down to me very stern and says, 'Look, I don't mind you making up Minbari words. Just don't use any of your damn album-cover names again!' It's not like we're talking about Tom Petty and the Heartbreakers here. It's not like the Jenerators are tearing up the *Billboard* charts! We're more or less a culty little novelty project that sells a handful of thousands of units and doesn't get a lot of attention. I said, 'I can't believe you knew that,' and he's like 'I know everything' and just walked away."

Joe Straczynski describes "Eyes" as a catchall for the season because of the way it underlines some of the issues explored in the first year. It allowed viewers who came to the show late to catch up on some of the stories that they had missed and encapsulated one of the main themes of *Babylon 5*, that every action has its consequences. "It showed there are consequences for all the things that Sinclair did to beat the system," says Joe. "They were not missed. They were noticed, and there comes a time when you have to pay the price for that. Throughout the show, that's what happens with all the characters: a price has to be paid."

17
"Legacies"

Cast
Commander Jeffrey Sinclair ....Michael O'Hare
Lt. Commander Susan Ivanova ....Claudia Christian
Security Chief Michael Garibaldi ....Jerry Doyle
Ambassador Delenn ....Mira Furlan
Dr. Stephen Franklin ....Richard Biggs
Talia Winters ....Andrea Thompson
Vir Cotto ....Stephen Furst
Lennier ....Bill Mumy
Na'Toth ....Caitlin Brown
Ambassador G'Kar ....Andreas Katsulas
Ambassador Londo Mollari ....Peter Jurasik

Guest Stars
Shai Alit Neroon ....John Vickery
Alisa Beldon ....Grace Una
Tech. No. 2 ....Joshua Cox
Security Man ....Richard Henry
Cart Owner ....Patrick O'Brien
Tech. No. 1 ....Marianne Robertson

"Thief!" shouts a cart owner in the Zocalo, as a girl flees through the crowd with jewelry taken from his stall.

The girl stops suddenly, screaming and clutching her hands to her head. She collapses on the floor, where Talia Winters rushes to her side. "She's just taken a mind burst," she says.

The girl, Alisa Beldon, is a telepath. She was struck down by a sudden rush of telepathic messages that still echo inside her mind. Talia helps her control the cacophony of voices and reassures her that the Psi Corps will help her deal with her talent. But Ivanova is determined that is not going to happen.

The jumpgate flares to life, and a Minbari ship enters Babylon 5 space. "A war cruiser," says Sinclair under his breath. "Never thought I'd see one of those again." It brings back memories of the Battle of the Line, when he fought against the Minbari. It is a point of obvious antagonism between him and Neroon, the leader of the war cruiser. Neroon is a member of the warrior caste and has come to honor Branmer, the Shai Alit who fought against Sinclair on the Line. They are displaying his body to every Minbari, but when they perform the ceremony on Babylon 5, his coffin is empty.

Neroon is furious. "To lose the vessel of his soul will bring his clan's fury on you," he tells Sinclair. Delenn calms him by insisting the Humans should be allowed to carry out an investigation. Garibaldi searches everywhere, even pumping the stomachs of the carrion-eating Pak'ma'ra, but finds no trace of the dead Minbari war leader.

Na'Toth tries to persuade the young telepath Alisa that she will be handsomely rewarded if she travels to Narn and gives up genetic samples to create a new breed of Narn telepaths. Alisa looks into Na'Toth's mind and touches something cold, ugly, and alien. She shrinks away. She has some dark choices—the Psi Corps, the drugs, or the Narn. But Ivanova believes there is another option and takes her to see Delenn. As they talk, Alisa gets a flash from Delenn's mind. Robed figures stun two Minbari guards and approach a coffin . . . Delenn quickly closes down her mind, but Alisa has seen enough. "Is there something going on around here about a dead body?" she asks.

Alisa tells Sinclair what she saw. He and Garibaldi interrupt Delenn as she makes preparations to send something back to Minbar. Sinclair takes the object from her and unwraps it to reveal a casket of ashes. Delenn confesses she arranged for the Shai Alit's body to be stolen because she knew him before he was a war leader, when he served as part of the religious caste. He never wanted to be a monument to war.

Delenn uses her authority as a member of the Grey Council to placate Neroon and orders him to apologize

*to Commander Sinclair. Neroon is surprised when it
provokes Sinclair to offer to send a message to Minbar,
praising Branmer for his valor and leadership in battle.
Neroon smiles. "You talk like a Minbari, Commander,"
he says.*

*Alisa decides to take Delenn's offer to go to Minbar,
where she can be an instrument of communication
between Humans and Minbari, and Ivanova and Talia
agree that she will be all right. Finally, she thanks
Sinclair and tells him that she saw one other thing in
Delenn's mind: "Chrysalis." Sinclair ponders the word
to himself as he watches her leave.*

"Legacies" was written by D. C. Fontana and was the only script from a freelancer in the first season that wasn't based on an assigned premise. "After I had done 'The War Prayer,' Joe said, 'We'd like you to do another one,' " says Dorothy. "I came in with this idea—actually, I had a couple of others—but this was the one they liked. Joe and Larry said, 'Okay, go with that.' Later on, much later on, they had a story that they wanted me to do, but they threw that one out in favor of 'Legacies,' because they liked 'Legacies' so much."

The focus of the episode is the young telepath and how the emergence of her talent suddenly opens a host of new opportunities for her. At the point Talia finds her in the Zocalo, she is little more than an urchin girl, forced to forage for herself in order to survive. The experience has turned her into a strong and spirited youngster, prepared to stand up for herself, even as Talia and Ivanova fight over her future. Originally, Alisa was supposed to have been around fifteen years old, hence the reference to her talent being triggered by the onset of puberty, but because of the restrictions on using child actors and the central role of the character, an older actress was cast.

Alisa comes across as an established character in her own right, but the purpose of the episode was more to bring out the other characters than to tell her story. "I thought it was very useful because it put the Ivanova and Talia relationship into the foreground," says Joe Straczynski. "We had been dancing around it here and there, but now for the first time, we got it and opened it up in front. And we learned a lot about the Psi Corps, and that knowledge would become important later on. There's some nice dynamics going into how the telepathic impulse works, so it covered a lot of good backstory ground for us."

Talia and Ivanova's battle over what should happen to Alisa becomes a personal one for them. At one point, their argument degenerates into personal abuse as Talia mentions Ivanova's mother and Ivanova responds by bringing up Jason Ironheart. It forces together two characters who would otherwise have as little as possible to do with each other, revealing their ideologies and bringing them into conflict. In the end, their opinions have little bearing on what Alisa decides for her future, but both can see that she will be all right with the Minbari. It is an important step in their relationship as they apologize to each other and agree to share a cup of coffee.

"Underlying that is the whole sexual attraction," says Andrea Thompson who plays Talia Winters. "I think both of them are ice queens: they very much needed friends. And both of them, I think, are fighting to keep a sense of authority in what's still essentially a guy's world."

The character of the Narns is also brought out by the arrival of Alisa, as Na'Toth tries to persuade her to go back to their homeworld, where her genetic material can be used to help create Narn telepaths. The issue of Narn telepaths goes right back to the pilot, when G'Kar tried to persuade Lyta Alexander to mate with him for the same reason, and forward to the third season, when it is revealed why there are no telepaths among the Narn. It was originally going to be G'Kar who made Alisa an offer she couldn't refuse, but it was changed because Andreas Katsulas was not available for that episode.

"I had a discussion with Joe on that one," says Julie Caitlin Brown, who played Na'Toth in the first season. "I said, 'You know, I don't think Na'Toth would say it this way. It was originally written for G'Kar, and it sounds like G'Kar's lines.' That was the only time I really disagreed with Joe and said, 'Gee, you know, I'd like to change this because I don't think Na'Toth would have said that.' But he said, 'No, I really need these lines to be said, and the fact that it's you and not G'Kar, I still think it will be okay.' I always felt a little funny about that, because I never saw her as a conniver. She's so straightforward. G'Kar was a hustler, but I found Na'Toth as more . . . I mean, she'd kick your teeth in right in your face; she didn't go around the back at all."

Alisa is dissuaded from taking up the Narns' offer when she looks inside Na'Toth's mind and finds it "cold, ugly, and alien." "I think that's a Human interpretation of who the Narn are," says Julie. "Let's face it, we have red eyes. We have really tough spotted skin. It's not an easy planet, and it would frighten a little girl. It would be so different, and our minds are very passionate. There was a lot of anger in Na'Toth."

The other story brings up a lot of underlying emotion generated by the Earth–Minbari War. Sinclair said in "And the Sky Full of Stars" that he had to resist the urge to strangle Minbari with his bare hands for years after the war, and some of those feelings are reawakened when he sees a Minbari war cruiser come through the jumpgate. But the bulk of the hatred comes out of Neroon, a member of the warrior caste, who is angry over the war's conclusion. This feeds into the backstory of the Minbari surrender at the Battle of the Line and the warriors' resentment of the Grey Council's decision.

It also reflects on the split between the warrior and religious castes, which becomes more marked as the series progresses. Neroon is affronted when Delenn orders him to support her story that Branmer's body was miraculously transformed and to apologize to Sinclair. His resentment can be interpreted as an irritation at being dictated to by someone who is both a member of the Grey Council and the religious caste.

Branmer represents that dichotomy of the Minbari race. He is the war hero who was forced to put aside his religious vocation to serve in what Delenn calls the "Holy War

Against Earth." She feels that his wish for a simple funeral has been ignored by the warriors, who would rather use his body as a memorial to war.

"The story came to mind because I had been reading a book about Lincoln's funeral," says Dorothy Fontana. "It struck me that his body was laid out and paraded through Philadelphia and New York, all the way across the country to Springfield, and thousands of people wanted to see this slain president. His body was on display and everything. And that triggered to mind: 'Well, that's interesting. What about the Minbari? Would the Minbari do something like this for a fallen leader? And what about Delenn?' "

Since being introduced in "Legacies," Neroon, played by John Vickery, has become an important character in his own right. Mira Furlan, who plays Delenn, has fond memories of working alongside him. "It was fun to work with him," she says. "He's such a strong actor, and we had a lot of fun. Sometimes on film you get frustrated, because somehow you suppress your strength and it's all about subtleties and little things here and there, and sometimes I have such a feeling that I have to burst out and let it all go. John Vickery and Morgan Sheppard [the Soul Hunter] are the right persons to do it with. It's just like this theatrical outburst of energy, and I liked that."

Neroon finally faces Sinclair under Delenn's orders to apologize for his behavior. Sinclair's response is unexpected and surprises Neroon into forming a genuine reconciliation with him. They are both warriors whose battle is over. "It was an opportunity to meet and realize that they had more in common than not," says Michael O'Hare. "In fact, that scene meant very much to me when I played it. I said there had been enough war. He and I both dealt with each other with dignity and honor. That was the point of that scene."

Neroon's comment, "You talk like a Minbari, Commander," has more significance than is immediately apparent. It foreshadows the revelation still to come about Sinclair and is not the last we have heard of that sentence.

18
"A Voice in the Wilderness, Part One"

Cast

Commander Jeffrey Sinclair ....Michael O'Hare
Lt. Commander Susan Ivanova ....Claudia Christian
Security Chief Michael Garibaldi ....Jerry Doyle
Ambassador Delenn ....Mira Furlan
Dr. Stephen Franklin ....Richard Biggs
Talia Winters ....Andrea Thompson
Vir Cotto ....Stephen Furst
Lennier ....Bill Mumy
Na'Toth ....Caitlin Brown
Ambassador G'Kar ....Andreas Katsulas
Ambassador Londo Mollari ....Peter Jurasik

Guest Stars

Draal ....Louis Turenne
Varn ....Curt Lowens
Security Guard ....Craig Barnett
Derek Mobotabwe ....Langdon Bensing
EarthForce Liaison ....Kelly Coyle
Bartender ....Kathryn Cressida
Dr. Tasaki ....Jim Ishida
ISN Reporter ....Lenore Kasdorf
Tech. No. 1 ....Marianne Robertson
Psi Corps Rep ....Patty Toy
Technician ....Jerry Well

A beam of light shoots out from Epsilon 3, narrowly missing a survey shuttle and sending it tumbling toward the planet. The world that Babylon 5 orbits is not as cold and dead as was once thought.

Delenn turns and a huge smile breaks out across her face. "Draal!" she says, facing her old mentor and teacher. She welcomes him into her quarters, but the news he brings is not news she wants to hear. Their homeworld of Minbar is drifting, he tells her, and he is going to the sea. "Then when you leave here, I will never see you again," she says sadly.

Trouble has erupted on Mars. Rioting has engulfed the Earth colony, and communications have been cut off. Garibaldi is infuriated, shouting at the EarthForce liaison to let him get a signal through, but it does him no good. So he turns to Talia Winters and tells her about the woman he met on Mars, Lise Hampton. Their relationship was so serious, they even talked about marriage, but when he was offered a job on Babylon 5 and she refused to go with him, it ended in a bitter row. Since then he'd often thought of calling her but never did. "I can't sleep not knowing if she's okay," he tells Talia. "You're my last hope."

The survey ship is targeted by a hail of missiles as soon as it touches the planet's surface. It is only saved by a barrage of fire sent from Babylon 5, which confuses the missiles' target systems. Ivanova considers the attack a threat to station security, and Sinclair considers it a possible first-contact situation. "I'd say we pretty much have to go down there and check it out," he says. "Wouldn't you agree, Lieutenant Commander?"

Sinclair and Ivanova are in a shuttle heading for the planet. Three missiles are fired from deep within the planet, and Babylon 5's ships respond with a rain of fire. The shuttle avoids the missiles and accelerates deep into the planet's core.

Sinclair and Ivanova step out into a dark cavern, the bright beams of their searchlights cutting through the blackness to reveal the burned and tattered remains of a spacesuit. Sinclair picks up a rock and throws it toward the suit. It triggers a booby trap, and the passageway lights up with a crisscross of laser beams. Sinclair throws another rock, waits for the beams to fire, then in the three seconds it takes them to recharge, he and Ivanova make a run for it, laser light erupting behind them. They dive to the ground, barely escaping intact.

*They turn a corner and see before them a spectacle of
technology they could hardly dream of. Alien circuitry
towers above them and stretches out into infinity below
them. Bolts of light shoot past them, and parts of the
machine, like transport tubes in a giant building, glide
up and down on either side. Awestruck, they step onto
the narrow bridge that lies before them. As they walk,
they look like two tiny specks in a far greater universe.*

*A flickering image of an alien appears before them.
"Help me . . . ," he calls out in a weak voice. He turns to
his right and disappears. Sinclair and Ivanova follow his
lead and enter a chamber bathed in orange light. The
glow comes from a pulsating mass of biomechanical
technology radiating onto the walls, and at its center is
the alien. "Help me," he says weakly, "or your people—
all your people—will die."*

"**A** Voice in the Wilderness" is one of the major arc
episodes of the first season, introducing the Great
Machine on Epsilon 3, but it was originally going to be told in
only one part. "Warners made the point that if we made a
two-part episode, we could get some additional money,"
says Joe Straczynski. "My sense was that wherever we
could possibly help the production values of the show—if by
doing this we could make the show better—I was happy to
do it. So, in this case it came down to 'Can I make this story
expand and fill two hours?' And looking at it, I felt there was
enough there, so I broke it up into two parts."

A lot of the extra resources went into building sets, in particular those on Epsilon 3 comprising the Machine and the
many tunnels leading to it. "They spent a lot of money on
that set," says Michael O'Hare. "It looked pretty realistic
when you were in it. The color of the rock was very reddish,
which is a little unusual, but it was a fairly believable place to
be in."

Sinclair and Ivanova go down to the planet, clearly itching
to get off the station and see a bit of action. The action they
see involves running for their lives and diving for cover as

laser beams shoot out of the rocks. "Most of that stuff was done by stunt people," reveals Claudia Christian, who plays Ivanova. "It's kind of uncomfortable when you're shooting on Stage B, where a lot of Down-Below is and where Epsilon 3 is. It's kind of depressing—it's always dirty. I remember it wasn't a very pleasant week. Not as much for me as the crew who were there. They're the ones who don't have much opportunity to leave the set. I have, of course, time to go to my trailer. They're constantly breathing in that junk. You're constantly fatigued, and it's not my fondest, cleanest memory of *Babylon 5*."

The dust and muck are added to when the seismic activity inside the planet causes an avalanche, sending rocks and dust tumbling on top of Sinclair and Ivanova. "To tell you the truth, that got a little dangerous," says Michael O'Hare. "There was one time it fell when it wasn't supposed to fall, and, Styrofoam rocks or not, it was still quite something. I have almost no physical fear. I don't know why. It's nothing to brag about. For some reason, I don't have a lot of it. I have other things, but those things don't bother me, so I thought it was funny. Grown people running around pretending to hide from rays coming out of the side of Styrofoam rocks! You've got to have a sense of humor, for God's sake."

There was a lot of humor in the first part of "A Voice in the Wilderness." One of the scenes, of Londo explaining his bafflement at why Humans sing the Hokey-Pokey to their children, was originally going to be in the second episode, but it was moved when the first episode ran short.

"I don't know what to say about that," says Peter Jurasik (Londo). "I've been so complimentary to Joe about adding challenges and facets to character, then on occasions you'll open the script and you think, 'This can't really be happening; this has to be like a birthday joke!' When I read that I thought, 'I don't actually have to do this?' We talked in 'Parliament of Dreams' about letting go and just jumping in, and I'm afraid the Hokey-Pokey had that aspect to it, to actually get your courage up. It was actually a lot easier for me to take that beautiful Italian girl in my arms and kiss her [in

'Born to the Purple'] than it was for me to stand up in front of the crew and sing the Hokey-Pokey. But we do our best, and they're paying me to act, so act I must."

Another fun scene is when Talia tells Sinclair that Garibaldi seems always to be waiting for her whenever she takes the transport tube. This gag had been set up through several previous episodes, most memorably in "Mind War" when she senses Garibaldi's thoughts and elbows him in the stomach. Of course, on this occasion, the transport tube doors open to reveal Garibaldi standing there grinning like the proverbial Cheshire cat.

"The thing with Garibaldi and Talia was—it was the cat and mouse," says Jerry Doyle. "It was the little boy and the girl, it was playful, it was fun, it was intended. The thing that I read on Garibaldi with Talia's character was that this was somebody really different and really special—it wasn't just somebody else—and he pursued it. He saw something there, and there was a side of Garibaldi that you weren't going to see unless it was in a place where he felt safe and where he wasn't going to be judged. He could let down his guard, and for whatever reason, that character sparked that kind of reaction when she was with him."

That is very much the case when Garibaldi approaches Talia for help in trying to find Lise, the girlfriend he left on Mars. The side of the story concerning the Mars riots widens the action, shedding light on another sector of the galaxy and feeding into the unrest back home, with the Free Mars and Homeguard terrorist movements already established in "Mind War," "Eyes," and others. "You want to convey the sense of a big story, that more is happening than what we see in front of us," says the writer, Joe Straczynski. "The trick is to point to an ice cube floating in the water and imply an iceberg. What I try and do is keep certain threads alive and keep you aware that there is Mars, there is Minbar, there is Earth, and by comparing the places that we know I think we make the show more real by doing that. And again, of course, Mars would take on greater preeminence later on and particularly in the fourth season."

The action is all very remote in "A Voice in the Wilderness," but it is brought home to the audience because of Garibaldi's connection with Mars. "Right. You can't just drag in Mars philosophically," says Joe. "You have to have some kind of tie to it that makes us care about what is going on. It also gave me the chance to explore Michael [Garibaldi]'s background as a character himself and the things he's gone through to get where he is and the tragic side of his character. It was the chance to do a lot of things in a small amount of space."

Garibaldi finds himself trapped on the station, unable to do anything about the anxiety that is eating him up inside. As he is considering his predicament, sitting at the bar nursing a glass of water, Londo approaches him and tries to cheer him up. The relationship between Londo and Garibaldi is a fascinating one because they are so different on the surface. One is Human, the other is Centauri; one has a responsible job, the other would rather spend his life drinking and gambling. And yet they have something in common.

"I don't see it as a drunk and an ex-drunk," says Jerry Doyle. "I don't see it as a drinker sitting there wishing he had a drink, and I don't see it as a drinker sitting there feeling guilty about having a drink. I played those as two people who kinda had a handle on each other and in all the craziness and all the nonsense could actually sit down and have a conversation. Two guys who are kinda on the out: Londo's a fading ruler in a crumbling empire, and Garibaldi is a crumbling figure to a certain degree, with vices and getting fired and getting transferred and losing friends and relationships. So they both do share certain things, and that's how I played the relationship."

The episode was originally going to end with Varn telling Sinclair and Ivanova that unless they help him, everyone on Babylon 5 will be destroyed. But because the episode was a little short, some scenes were shifted over from the second episode, and it ended with the action freezing as a large ship is about to enter through the jumpgate instead.

19
"A Voice in the Wilderness, Part Two"

Cast

Commander Jeffrey Sinclair ....Michael O'Hare
Lt. Commander Susan Ivanova ....Claudia Christian
Security Chief Michael Garibaldi ....Jerry Doyle
Ambassador Delenn ....Mira Furlan
Dr. Stephen Franklin ....Richard Biggs
Talia Winters ....Andrea Thompson
Vir Cotto ....Stephen Furst
Lennier ....Bill Mumy
Na'Toth ....Caitlin Brown
Ambassador G'Kar ....Andreas Katsulas
Ambassador Londo Mollari ....Peter Jurasik

Guest Stars

Draal ....Louis Turenne
Varn ....Curt Lowens
Captain Ellis Pierce ....Ron Canada
Lise Hampton ....Denise Gentile
Senator Hidoshi ....Aki Aleong
Tech. No. 2 ....Joshua Cox
Rowdy No. 1 ....Chip Heller
ISN Reporter ....Lenore Kasdorf
Takarn ....Michelan Sisti
Tech. No. 1 ....Marianne Robertson

*An Earth cruiser bursts out of the jumpgate into
Babylon 5 space. "We're assuming control of this
station," says Captain Ellis Pierce. He has been ordered
to intervene by Planetary Security, who have read
Sinclair's report on the technology he found on Epsilon 3
and decided to seize it for Earth.*

Sinclair is furious. He even appeals to the Senate, but

the president is too "busy" to help. Plus the alien they brought up from the planet is dying in medlab, and the infrastructure of the planet is collapsing without him. If this continues, the planet will blow up, taking Babylon 5 with it.

Garibaldi looks at his stale piece of pizza and throws it back into the box. He's worried about Lise. All Talia's contacts at Psi Corps were able to find out is that she isn't on the list of survivors. His thoughts are interrupted by Sinclair, who's come to talk to him about his violent outburst in the Zocalo. Garibaldi stands and paces around the room. "I know, I know. It was stupid," he says. "What am I supposed to do? I've never felt this helpless before."

Draal hears a voice calling him. It is Varn, the alien from the planet. He is drawn to medlab, where Varn regains consciousness for a moment. "The planet below . . . do not land," he warns them. "Destroy you all . . . without the heart . . . without another . . ."

But Captain Pierce has every intention of landing, even though his ships have little hope of getting through the planet's defenses. Then the jumpgate fires up, and an alien fleet emerges. They are outcasts from Varn's race, who demand the planet for themselves. Before long the space around Babylon 5 is alight with laser fire.

A shuttle dodges the hail of blasts and heads for the planet. Londo is at the controls, laughing wildly, remembering his days as a young Centauri leading the raid on Fralis 12. His passengers, Draal, Delenn, and Varn, sit uncomfortably behind him.

Varn leads them to the heart of the planet and to the Great Machine he has been a part of for five hundred years. But he is dying, and it is time for "another" to take his place. Draal knows that he must be the one. "I came here looking for a reason," he says. "Here, I have found it." Draal climbs into the biomechanic connections and becomes part of the machine. Delenn looks up at him and says good-bye to her old friend.

A holographic image of Draal appears in C&C, and to Captain Pierce, and to the head of the alien fleet. He warns them all to stay away. "The secrets buried here must remain secret," he says. "When the time is right, we will be here waiting for you."

A link to Mars is at last established and patched through to Garibaldi. He smiles when he sees Lise's face. She is wounded but otherwise fine. He stumbles through a speech about getting back together, but she cuts him off with the news he least expected. "I can't," she tells him. "I'm married . . . We're expecting our first baby in September." Garibaldi's face falls. He tells her he's glad, but his expression displays his true feelings.

Garibaldi stands in the Sanctuary Room, looking out at the stars. He is joined by Delenn. He asks her why she didn't tell them about Varn. "Because if I had . . . Commander Sinclair would be the one down there," she says. "He is looking for a purpose . . . But his destiny lies elsewhere."

As soon as the Earth Alliance cruiser *Hyperion* arrives in Babylon 5 space, diplomacy goes straight out of the window. Earth's designs on the powerful technology, apparently there for the taking, have nothing to do with the reason the station was established in the first place and everything to do with self-interest.

"Isn't that typical, though?" says Joe Straczynski. "Every government gives lip service to diplomacy and getting along with each other, until they perceive that there is suddenly an advantage to be gained in throwing their weight around. And that's what they do. 'To hell with getting along—if we have technology hundreds of years ahead of everyone else, they have to get along with us.' So from the government's perspective, the same result is achieved. We can have peace by being nice with each other or by having the biggest gun in town. To them it's all the same."

The introduction of the Great Machine, and Draal's promise that it will be there when Babylon 5 needs it, is an obvious setup for future events. It leads the audience to assume it will play a major role in the Shadow War, which is precisely why it doesn't do that and instead becomes important during the fourth season. In "A Voice in the Wilderness," it is the *idea* of the Great Machine that is important. The sheer magnificence of the technology is what makes the biggest impact on both the characters and the audience.

"I always try to focus on the sense of wonder," says the writer, Joe Straczynski. "I like the idea of this vast alien structure that towers above us and below us. This goes back to the stories by Lovecraft and others, where you have your protagonist out among these—to use a Lovecraftian term—vast Cyclopean structures. Walking through these things—and we don't have anything like that here on this planet—gives you a real sense of power and awe. When someone from the countryside visits the big city for the first time, you tend to have them looking up at the big skyscrapers and going, 'Wow, wow, wow,' so how much more of a 'Wow' do you get if this structure is several miles deep?"

Draal's willingness to give up the rest of his life to become part of the machine is a self-sacrifice that comes from the Minbari's belief in being of service to others. It is a theme reiterated in several forms in the episode and throughout the series. "If there're any lessons or messages we try to convey in the show from time to time, this is one of them," says Joe. "In this country, coming out of the eighties and into the nineties, the emphasis tended to be on 'What can I get for myself?' and 'What can I do for me?' I felt that a different kind of message has to be sent from time to time, that there is equal value and importance in doing for others; and, yeah, some self-sacrifice may be involved or required, but that's required sometimes. If the country is invaded, if a friend is in need, you have to do what you have to do."

Delenn says at the end of the episode that, if she had told Sinclair about the machine, he would have been the one to sacrifice himself for the station. It is something proven time and again about the character, going back to Garibaldi's speech in "Infection," in which he talked about Sinclair looking for something worth dying for, and forward to his transition into Valen. "I identify with that," says Michael O'Hare, who plays Sinclair. "It's very funny about leadership, that people always think it's glamorous and a lot of fun and everyone's kissing your behind, and it's anything but that. That's the outer appearance at times, but good leadership is a job of service and self-sacrifice. So it's in keeping with that that Sinclair would feel the responsibility would fall to him to put himself on the line."

The theme is also brought out by Londo's character. At first sight it is perhaps surprising that he would risk himself for Delenn, but this is actually a fundamental part of Londo, which he tends to hide behind his fun-loving exterior. Londo is a man who once fought for his people and is now side-lined on Babylon 5, very much like the crumbling Centauri Republic that once knew greatness. When he pilots the shuttle down to Epsilon 3, it allows him to recapture his youth.

"What a scene that was," says Peter Jurasik with glee. "Boy, did we have fun! Somebody gave me a California map, and we ran a little film, with Londo having a big foldout road map, saying, 'Now, let's see, this is the Civic Center, and this is downtown . . .' That's a nice memory. We got to goof a lot with Londo, sitting up in the front seat and being the chauffeur. We do have a lot of laughs on the set. We're pretty loose at this point—we're downright crazy. It starts to get giddy down that end of the season, so we were having a good time."

Another character moment, which was quite small in terms of the episode, happens when Sinclair is taking off his jacket. Someone calls him on the link, and he gets his arm stuck in his sleeve. Michael O'Hare enjoyed that moment because it opened a chink in Sinclair's armor and allowed part of his character's Humanity to show through. "That was my idea," he says. "I was very often responsible for the more serious elements of the show. Other people could be irreverent or difficult and all of that sort of thing, and I often had the responsibility of reminding the audience that this is no joke, we're in outer space, we could all die any moment. And also I had a lot of expositional responsibilities, setting up the stories, explaining it, giving long speeches that are difficult to make dramatic. So there weren't many opportunities for humor for my character . . . I found my moments when I could, and one of them was right in the middle of this, where usually the commander would take off his jacket and throw it down and be in complete control, stride forward and make a decision. You see that on television or movies, and you say, 'Boy, I wish I took my coat off like that!' because in daily life we don't do that. So I purposely got my arm caught In the damn coat."

As the problems on Epsilon 3 are resolved and Captain Pierce expresses his "regrets" for overstepping his authority, things also begin to quiet down on Mars. Communication channels begin to come back on-line, and Garibaldi is finally able to speak to his former girlfriend, Lise. It is a tragic moment for the character as, after waiting so long to pluck up the courage to talk to her, he finds she is married and expecting a baby.

"Jerry and I talked about the degree of emotion he was going to reveal," remembers the director, Janet Greek. "I really wanted that to be an opportunity for him to show a more sensitive moment. He was looking for some way to give his character more color, and that served that really nicely."

"I thought it was well written," adds Jerry Doyle. "I thought it was a pretty good buildup to the point where we would ultimately not like to find ourselves in. 'I really screwed up, I made my mistakes, and God, here I am; I put my heart on my sleeve, and you're what?' And then you have to hide what's really going on inside you, so you put your bravado on, and you go into a 'Garibaldiism' and build the wall a little thicker and a little higher, not letting anybody get through and see that you're really hurt. Then you come at your next scene with a little bit of a different spin on it. So it's nice that they've laid in these elements of my character that I can carry with me from episode to episode."

Once the episodes were completed using the budget top-up promised by Warner Bros., it transpired that there would be no extra money, and the extra costs had to be borne by other parts of the production. So the whole raison d'être for turning "A Voice in the Wilderness" into a two-parter became obsolete.

20
"Babylon Squared"

Cast

Commander Jeffrey Sinclair ....Michael O'Hare
Lt. Commander Susan Ivanova ....Claudia Christian
Security Chief Michael Garibaldi ....Jerry Doyle
Ambassador Delenn ....Mira Furlan
Dr. Stephen Franklin ....Richard Biggs
Talia Winters ....Andrea Thompson
Vir Cotto ....Stephen Furst
Lennier ....Bill Mumy
Na'Toth ....Caitlin Brown
Ambassador G'Kar ....Andreas Katsulas
Ambassador Londo Mollari ....Peter Jurasik

Guest Stars

Major Krantz ....Kent Broadhurst
Zathras ....Tim Choate
Lise Hampton ....Denise Gentile
B4 Guard ....Frank Costa
Grey Council No. 2 ....,,,....Mark Hendrickson
Alpha Seven ....Doug E. McCoy
Panicked Man ...... ,,,.....................Tommy Rosales
Tech. No. 1 ....Marianne Robertson

Starfury pilot Alpha Seven stares openmouthed as a
shimmering shape of bright white emerges from the
space in front of him. Suddenly, the glow brightens,
consuming his cockpit with a white light. He cries out in
terror.

   An incoming signal confirms that what he sees is
Babylon 4, commanded by Major Krantz, who is
desperate to get his crew off the station. Sinclair and
Garibaldi lead a fleet of ships over to the station to
find that the whole place is unstable. As they stand in
the docking bay, there is a tremor and a white light

*flashes across Sinclair's face, pulling him into the
future.*

*Sinclair is on Babylon 5, Humans and aliens running
past him, security teams firing PPGs into the air. Beside
him is Garibaldi, scared, bloody, and bruised. "They've
burned through levels seven and eight . . . Can't stop
'em," he shouts over the sounds of fear and panic.
Sinclair stares at him, lost, confused. Garibaldi urges
him to go. "I finally understand," Garibaldi says. "This
is the moment I was born for." He fires wildly at the
unseen invaders as Sinclair is carried away by the tide of
escaping bodies.*

*The white light flashes Sinclair back to the present.
"It's different for everyone," Krantz says, "a flash-
forward or backward . . . we've become unstuck in
time."*

It was after one of these flashes, Krantz explains, that
they found an alien who calls himself Zathras. The alien
looks up as Krantz brings Sinclair and Garibaldi into his
room. He seems to recognize Sinclair, but then the look
fades and he shakes his head. "Not The One," he says.
Sinclair is nonplussed, but Zathras will only say he has
come to take Babylon 4 through time to fight in the
Great War.

Delenn enters the chamber of the Grey Council to
take her place as one of The Nine. She has been
summoned to become their new leader, but she refuses
because of the calling of her heart. "Valen said that the
Humans, and some among them, had a destiny," she
says. "It was my place to study them . . . I have not yet
finished that task." The Council votes that she may
return to Babylon 5, but her future as one of The Nine is
uncertain.

A quake rumbles through Babylon 4 as Sinclair,
Krantz, and Zathras try to make it to the docking bay.
Then another tremor, worse this time, shakes everything
and dislodges one of the structural beams. Zathras sees
it falling toward Sinclair and pushes him out of the way,

*taking the full force of the beam as it crashes down on
top of him. Sinclair tries to free him, but Zathras is
pinned to the ground. "Go," Zathras tells him. "You
have a destiny." Reluctantly, Sinclair runs after the
others.*

*Zathras senses someone else approach. He looks
up to see a figure in a blue spacesuit. The faceplate
is opaque, making it impossible to see who is inside.
"Zathras knew you would not leave him," he
says. "Zathras trusts The One."*

*A Grey Council member stops Delenn as she is about
to leave their ship. He gives her a triluminary, the
symbol of the Grey Council. "You will have more need
of it than we will," he says.*

*A figure in a blue spacesuit watches Sinclair's shuttle
depart from Babylon 4. He takes off his helmet to reveal
Sinclair, but it is an older Sinclair, whose hair has turned
gray and whose face is marked by a scar. "I tried to
warn them," he says, "but it all happened just the way I
remember it."*

"Babylon Squared" answers one of the great mysteries of
the Babylon 5 universe: what happened to Babylon 4?
But it does so by replacing that one simple question with many
more complex ones. Most of these would not be answered
until the two-parter in the third season, "War Without End." It
meant that writing the episode was an exercise in meticulous
planning.

"You have to tell one story but set everything in motion to
tell a second story that you won't tell for two years," says
Joe Straczynski. "It's like walking into somebody's house
and telling him the setup for a joke and coming back two
years later to tell him the punchline. You're banking a great
deal on the relative patience of your audience. So I knew it
had to be very difficult. And I had to also construct it on the
theory that I could do the whole second part in one episode
down the road."

Again, for an episode that has such a large dramatic

impact, it has some of the most memorable comedy moments of the first year. The episode begins with Sinclair and
Garibaldi fooling Ivanova into thinking she slept through
breakfast, while important plot information about the pilot
sent out to investigate tachyon emissions coming from
Sector 14 is slipped almost unnoticed into the dialogue. "If I
recall the scene correctly, it was hard," says Claudia Christian (Ivanova). "I think one of the most difficult things to play
in acting is surprise, because you can't be surprised. You can
be moved to tears because the moment is very real to you,
because you're listening to the words, and that is a real
response. Comedy is so much easier for me. I remember
having to scream during movies or getting killed or seeing
the murderer, and that was easier to me than having to feign
surprise at a surprise party. It always seems so funny
because you know it's in the script, you know it's coming,
you anticipate it, and you have to remove yourself."

Later on Garibaldi decides to pass the time of day in the
shuttle by asking Sinclair about the way he gets dressed in
the morning. On the one hand, this acknowledges that space
travel takes a long time, that it takes three hours to get to
Sector 14 in normal space, and on the other, it makes you
wonder whether you zip your fly first or fasten it first. "I had
the same reaction when I learned the scene," says Michael
O'Hare. "I thought, 'Now wait a minute—I never thought of
that. How do I do that?' "

The scenes on Babylon 4 looked very different from the
more familiar Babylon 5, even though it was filmed using the
same sets. "That was kind of tough," admits the director,
Jim Johnston. "Working with the production designer [John
Iacovelli], we changed the whole color scheme. I worked
hard to give it a sense of panic on the station, that everyone
was shell-shocked. I played everybody on the station like
they had seen ghosts and they didn't like it."

The flashes of time that made the Babylon 4 crew look so
shell-shocked added to the impact of the episode on many
levels. First, they added to the mystery of what is happening to the station and to the desperation of those on board.

Second, they allow for a wonderful scene between Garibaldi and his girlfriend, Lise. They had spoken over the com-channel in "A Voice in the Wilderness," but this is the only time we see them face-to-face. From the audience's perspective, it has a double impact because, even as she is saying good-bye to him, both the audience and Garibaldi know that she dumps him in favor of another man.

The flash-forward in Sinclair's case is more foreshadowing of the terrible events to come. "I never knew what the hell that scene meant—we just did it," says Michael O'Hare. "Joe Straczynski knows where he's going to take the story, but you're just doing the flashbacks. You're not sure what they mean, so you're just trying to play them as best you can."

The director, Jim Johnston, certainly had an idea of what the scene was about. It was Babylon 5 being overrun by Shadows, and that's what he filmed. "I wanted to show more of the enemy, and I filmed silhouettes of shadows on walls and things," he says. "I think they were pretty scary, but they never ended up in the picture. I guess Joe wanted to keep more of a mystery of who those people were. I also tried to make that scene bigger than scripted. Being overrun, like Vietnam, where you're just being swept away—that was the feeling I was trying to get there."

The compound effect of the time anomalies is pulling the station apart. This builds to one scene in which everything is collapsing around Sinclair, and he stands watching it, mesmerized, like a captain going down with his ship. It is, of course, Garibaldi who pulls him out of it. "I had fun shooting that," says Jerry Doyle, who plays Garibaldi. "They were throwing stuff onto the set, squibs were going off, and I remember picking up stuff and throwing it off camera. I remember the director picking up some of the stuff and throwing it back at me. Then I'd get pissed off and start throwing the stuff back again! It was fun to be on the set with the smoke and the steel and the explosions. It was an easy episode to shoot because it was so real."

Interwoven with the events on Babylon 4 is Delenn's visit

to the Grey Council. The plots parallel each other in the sense that they both answer long-standing questions only to replace them with greater mysteries. In Delenn's speech to the Grey Council, she reveals why she is on Babylon 5, but her resolve to stay there and fulfill the prophecy lays down a whole set of new mysteries. This one thing is so important to her that she is prepared to reject tradition, defy the others, and refuse to lead them. "Because she's in touch with Valen, because she knows more than any of them, and because she is loyal to that knowledge," explains Mira Furlan (Delenn). "She has knowledge that none of those Grey Council members have, so that's her mission. And it's repeated, it's like a motif for my character, I have a destiny which comes in in 'The Inquisitor' and so on. I have a destiny, the prophecy, my mission, my task, my place in the universe. I like that thought. I wish I could think that of my own place."

This episode prepares Delenn for some of the changes that are to come. In being given the triluminary, she is given the means to begin her transformation in "Chrysalis," and in standing against the Grey Council, she is prepared for their rejection of her in the second season.

Perhaps the biggest mystery to be set up in "Babylon Squared" is: What does Zathras mean by "The One"? And who is in the spacesuit? Several clues are laid in throughout the episode, beginning with the moment the figure appears, phasing in and out in Babylon 4's Central Corridor. Sinclair reaches out to him and is blown backward. "That was a stuntman," says Michael O'Hare. "The way they did that was they had a belt around him and a hook that hooked onto the back of the belt, and the line went way up high to a set of pulleys, and the camera cut the line out of the frame so you didn't see it, and they just all at once pulled him and he just went [through the air], then it looks like he was shot backward by an electrical charge. The reality is that's me touching myself—if you pardon the expression!"

But is it? When we see the spacesuited figure remove his helmet, we see an older Sinclair, and this appears to answer the immediate mystery. The question then becomes: Why does Zathras call him "The One"? And what has happened to Sinclair in the intervening time? It is a question that isn't answered until "War Without End," which expertly upsets many of the assumptions set up in "Babylon Squared." Then the mystery becomes: What was originally planned before it was known that Michael O'Hare would be leaving the series? And that is a mystery that may never be answered.

21
"The Quality of Mercy"

Cast

Commander Jeffrey Sinclair ....Michael O'Hare
Lt. Commander Susan Ivanova ....Claudia Christian
Security Chief Michael Garibaldi ....Jerry Doyle
Ambassador Delenn ....Mira Furlan
Dr. Stephen Franklin ....Richard Biggs
Talia Winters ....Andrea Thompson
Vir Cotto ....Stephen Furst
Lennier ....Bill Mumy
Na'Toth ....Caitlin Brown
Ambassador G'Kar ....Andreas Katsulas
Ambassador Londo Mollari ....Peter Jurasik

Guest Stars

Dr. Laura Rosen ....June Lockhart
Janice Rosen ....Kate McNeil
Karl Mueller ....Mark Rolston
Centauri Senator ....Damian London
Ombuds Wellington ....Jim Norton
Rose ....Lynn Anderson
Lurker ....Phillippe Bergeron
Second Guard ....David L. Crowley
Guard ....Kevin McBride
Young Woman Patient ....Constance Zimmer

Instead of going to Dr. Franklin's unofficial clinic in Down-Below, lurkers have started seeing an unlicensed doctor, Laura Rosen. She claims to be able to heal any ailment by simply plugging a patient into one end of an alien machine and herself into the other. "Does the term con job ring a bell?" Franklin asks her.

Talia Winters takes a black band from a box on her dressing table and places it across her Psi Corps badge.

*She is to scan Karl Mueller, a murderer sentenced to
brainwipe.*

Talia faces Mueller across the table and peers into his
mind. There she sees herself standing opposite Mueller in
a kind of limbo. Behind him, figures emerge from the
darkness. They are all the people he has killed. One after
another, more and more. She pulls out of his mind in
terror and staggers back from him. The horror is so
much, she can barely stand.

*Franklin secretly monitors Laura Rosen as she
performs one of her treatments and discovers the
machine is transferring life energy from her to her
patients. He knows it is killing her, but she doesn't care.
She is suffering from Lake's Syndrome. She's dying
anyway.*

*Londo is introducing Lennier to poker, but Lennier is
too honest to make a good gambler, so Londo decides to
improve the odds a little. He lets a tentacle wriggle out
from under his clothes and surreptitiously reach for the
pack of cards. At the same time, a gambler opposite him
puts a jug of iced water on the table, trapping Londo's
tentacle beneath it. Londo shivers as the tentacle tries to
wriggle free. The gambler looks down and sees what is
going on. He lifts the jug and—snap!—the tentacle
retracts into Londo's body. The gambler punches Londo,
and the room erupts into a brawl.*

*Mueller, flanked by Garibaldi and two guards, is
taken to be brainwiped. They stop at a transport tube,
and Mueller seizes his chance. He elbows Garibaldi in
the face and dives into the tube. Garibaldi reaches for
his PPG and fires a shot. It burns through Mueller's arm,
and Mueller falls to his knees as the transport tube doors
close and carry him away.*

*Franklin, realizing Mueller will need medical
treatment, runs to Laura Rosen to warn her. When he
gets there, he finds Mueller already linked up to the
machine and holding Laura's daughter hostage. Franklin
steps forward, but Mueller fires his PPG, striking the
wall by Franklin's arm. "The next shot will not miss," he*

*says. Laura believes him and, realizing she has no
choice, reaches for the controls on the machine. The
energy flow reverses, pulling the life force out of Mueller
in a rush that makes him helpless. He buckles with the
pain of her Lake's Syndrome as the machine drains every
drop of life from his body. He falls to the floor, dead.*

*A rather embarrassed Londo and Lennier face Sinclair
to explain their behavior in the club. Lennier takes full
responsibility, which totally astonishes Londo. After
Sinclair has gone, he asks why. "In Minbari culture,"
Lennier explains, "we are taught that it is an honor to
help another save face."*

*The court decides that Laura Rosen acted in self-
defense and rules she is free to go as long as she hands
the machine over to station personnel. Dr. Franklin is
looking forward to studying it. "Who knows?" he says.
"It might be able to preserve someone's life when
nothing else works."*

"The Quality of Mercy" is perhaps most memorable as
the show that featured one of Londo's penises. "To
actually have your genitalia as part of the script is really a
wonderful thing," says Peter Jurasik.

The idea came out of Joe Straczynski's fevered brain
while he was suffering from a bout of flu. "I have no recollec-
tion whatsoever of writing the damn thing!" he says. "I know
I wrote it because my name is on it, and it showed up, and
everyone told me that I wrote it, I think as an article of faith
more than anything else. There were a couple of scripts that
I wrote when I was in that condition ['A Voice in the Wilderness' was also affected], and this is the one that I remember
the least. It's usually the case the more that I am under the
weather, the more bizarre my scripts tend to get."

The concept of Londo's six tentacular attributes came out
of a desire to make the Centauri less Human than they
seemed from outward appearances. "The prop women who
were there at the time had far too much fun at my expense
designing these things," says Joe. "They were always coming to me with different versions of that end piece and ask-

ing, 'Should it be diamond shape or spade shape? Should it be thinner or thicker? Should it have veins or no veins?' You just wanted them to go away and leave you alone and never come back—they were really enjoying my discomfort!"

This translated onto the set when it actually came to the filming. "It made everyone scream and squiggle and squirm," remembers Peter Jurasik. "The Optic Nerve [special effects] people would come on and bring in this big long tentacle thing, and they'd have to wet it down, and it was kind of gooey and 'Who's going to touch it?' and 'I don't want to pick it up, you pick it up,' that kind of stuff. It made it a lot of fun. But talk about another interesting aspect to the character! What else do you want but six extra organs that you can reach under the table and steal your opponent's cards with?"

The episode took an unusual turn by pairing Londo and Lennier, two characters who would not normally have anything much to do with each other. It shows the versatility of *Babylon 5* that after twenty episodes there are still characters that haven't been put together and can send the story off in new directions. "They're wonderful characters to put side by side," says Peter. "It's an extra spice. You know you find a taste in a stew or a pudding or something, and you say, 'Hmm, what is that?' That's what was nice about seeing Londo and Lennier together. It was a really interesting taste in the whole stew to have."

Despite the obvious fun nature of the material, filming the episode was one of the most tense experiences of the whole season. It was the week after the massive North Ridge earthquake that shocked Los Angeles. "There was just a zillion aftershocks, and the lights were shaking; it was a very scary environment," says Bill Mumy, who plays Lennier.

It was an important episode for him because it established a lot about his background, that he grew up in a temple and knew no other life until he came to Babylon 5. But it also reveals something surprising about Lennier, that when challenged he can fight like an expert. "That was filmed on my fortieth birthday," says Bill. "My son—who was, like, four at that time—was there that day. My wife and my son came down, and it was great. Here I am celebrating my fortieth birthday, and I get to be an action hero!"

Bill Mumy provides a behind-the-scenes link to the other side of the plot, where June Lockhart was playing Dr. Laura Rosen. Her background in the science fiction genre comes from *Lost in Space*, in which she played Maureen Robinson, the mother of Bill's character, Will Robinson. "I begged everybody—we both begged—to do a scene together," says Bill. "I wanted to be a Human in the background in the scene. I wanted to be a security guard or a medlab guy, just be able to walk past her and give her that look, 'Don't I know you?' and carry on."

It never happened, partly because of the problems with the earthquake and partly because the *Lost in Space* connection would detract from the episode. Instead, most of June Lockhart's scenes were with Richard Biggs's Dr. Franklin. "What a breath of fresh air June was," he says. "It rained in Southern California that particular episode, and there was a beautiful rainbow one day while we were shooting. We were behind schedule, the director was under a lot of pressure, we were all watching the clock and hurry, hurry, hurry, and June happened to go outside for a minute, and—*boom!*—there was this beautiful rainbow. She came back to the set and said, 'Everyone, stop. Let's go look at the rainbow.' And, believe it or not, everyone put their stuff down. You've got sixty people outside, and we all just sat there for two or three minutes, marveling at this rainbow that went from one horizon to the other."

June Lockhart's character, Laura, showed compassion by the way she gave of her life energy to heal others. Lennier showed compassion when he took the blame for the fight that erupted in the club after he went gambling with Londo. And the quality-of-mercy theme is expanded in the treatment of the serial killer whom Talia has to scan. It raises the central question of whether it is more merciful to kill the man's personality by subjecting him to brainwipe, to execute him, or to put him in prison. "The science fiction writer's job is to try and extrapolate into the future and say how things might be done a hundred years or two hundred years from now," says Joe Straczynski. "Here's a notion of a form of capital punishment which, in essence, leaves the body fully functional but destroys the personality. Is that actually death or not? What's the morality here?"

"That was a chilling episode," says Andrea Thompson, whose character had to perform the telepathic scan prior to the brainwipe. "I tried to get across the weight of this issue. As heinous as it is for someone to take anyone else's life— serial killers, like this guy was, child molesters, or anybody who does that sort of thing—I don't have a lot of compassion for them as a person, but at the same time, do you want to be the executioner? I think there are a lot of people who are for the death penalty, even now, but I wonder how many of those people would be willing to pull the switch. That's basically what Talia was being asked to do."

Talia found the experience so horrific that, when the scan was finished and she pulled out of his mind, she would have collapsed if two security guards hadn't been there to catch her. That reaction was different from the one in the script, which called on her to scream. "I have a great deal of difficulty screaming. It's not what happens to me when I'm afraid," says Andrea. "I've been in a couple of life-threatening situations. I was in a plane crash in 1983; I didn't scream . . . That's when I talked to Lorraine [Senna Ferrara], who I worked with before on *Falcon Crest*. She's a lovely director, and I said, 'I don't think a scream is appropriate here. It's that whole horrifying thing of looking into something like this, and what comes out is much more primal.' We discussed that, and I had to fight over that one. They wanted me to scream, and I think women are stronger than that."

The two plots marry when Mueller holds Laura Rosen at gunpoint and demands to be healed. When she is forced to reverse the flow of the life energy through the alien machine, their roles are also reversed. She becomes the killer, and he becomes the healer. And, even though everyone said she did the right thing, it is something that will weigh on her mind forever.

22
"Chrysalis"

Cast

Commander Jeffrey Sinclair ....Michael O'Hare
Lt. Commander Susan Ivanova ....Claudia Christian
Security Chief Michael Garibaldi ....Jerry Doyle
Ambassador Delenn ....Mira Furlan
Dr. Stephen Franklin ....Richard Biggs
Talia Winters ....Andrea Thompson
Vir Cotto ....Stephen Furst
Lennier ....Bill Mumy
Na'Toth ....Caitlin Brown
Ambassador G'Kar ....Andreas Katsulas
Ambassador Londo Mollari ....Peter Jurasik

Guest Stars

Catherine Sakai ....Julia Nickson
Garibaldi's Aide ....Macaulay Bruton
Lurker No. 1 ....Liz Burnette
Devereaux ....Edward Conery
News Anchor ....Maggie Egan
Senator ....Cheryl Francis Harrington
Narn Pilot ....Mark Hendrickson
Med. Tech ....James Kiriyama-Lem
Paramedic ....Wesley Leong

*A lurker stumbles through the crowd in the Zocalo,
clutching at his ribs with bloody fingers. Garibaldi turns
as the lurker takes two more steps and collapses in his
arms. "They're going to kill him," he murmurs. The
lurker passes out and never regains consciousness.*

*Sinclair's eyes avoid Catherine Sakai as words tumble
out of his mouth with no direction and little meaning.
Eventually, he realizes what he is doing, stops, and looks
directly at her. "Look," he says, "do you want to get
married or don't you?" She smiles back. "Yes."*

Londo meets Morden in the garden, his thoughts troubled by Narn–Centauri skirmishes around Quadrant 37. "We can fix it for you," says Morden. Londo laughs, but Morden is not joking.

A huge spidery vessel as dark as a shadow and covered in speckles of light appears out of nowhere around Quadrant 37. It blasts a Narn cruiser into pieces with a single energy beam. In seconds the sector is swarming with Shadow ships, blasting every Narn cruiser in sight, lighting up space with a deadly display of energy beams and explosions. Then the barrage of fire turns to the moonbase below, each strike creating a pattern of destruction.

Londo, aghast at what has happened, demands to see Morden. "You killed ten thousand Narns!" he says. Morden is taken aback. "I didn't know you cared," he says. "Your name is being spoken at the highest levels of the Centauri government . . . You're a hero."

Delenn holds up the triluminary to Sinclair and asks if he recognizes it. Sinclair is hit by a flash of memory of when the Minbari Grey Council captured and tortured him. "There are things you should know," Delenn says. "Come to my quarters, and I will tell you as much as I can. But do not wait too long, Commander."

Garibaldi finds out whom the dead lurker had been working for and traces the cargo he had been loading. It contains transmitters designed to jam EarthForce communications. Garibaldi pieces it all together and suddenly realizes whom they are going to kill. He runs to tell Sinclair, but a gang of men stand in his way. Garibaldi pulls his PPG on them, but the sound of a PPG blast comes from behind him. Garibaldi's face contorts in pain and astonishment as phased plasma burns into his back. He drops to the floor, revealing his aide standing behind him with a freshly discharged PPG in his hand.

Garibaldi is rushed to medlab. In a haze of pain and

*half-conscious, he grabs at Sinclair and pulls him close.
"They're going to kill . . . ," he gasps, ". . . the
president." Garibaldi loses consciousness, and Dr.
Franklin's team rushes in to try to save him.*

*Sinclair tries to get a message through to the
president, but every communications link is being
jammed. They patch ISN into C&C and hear the news
they were all fearing. The president's ship has exploded.*

*Kosh finds Sinclair sitting wearily at the Zocalo bar.
"You have forgotten something," he says. Sinclair
realizes in a moment and rushes to Delenn's quarters,
but he is too late. At the far end, attached to the wall, is
a mass of fibers forming a chrysalis. Through the
interlaced webbing he can just make out Delenn's face.
"She is changing," says Lennier.*

*Sinclair sits in his quarters, staring into space.
Catherine puts her head on his chest, but he hardly
notices. He is thinking about Quadrant 37, Garibaldi,
and Delenn. "Nothing's the same anymore," he says.*

Everything in *Babylon* 5's first season builds toward
"Chrysalis." The conflict between the Narns and the
Centauri, political unrest on Earth, the prophecy Delenn
believes she is following, Sinclair's troubled love life, and the
mystery over his missing twenty-four hours at the Battle of
the Line all come to a head in this episode. Joe Straczynski
laid the threads throughout the season and, as he says,
pulled them into a knot in "Chrysalis." It seems that all the
characters are now falling headlong into darkness. "There's
always a sense that the characters can control it, can stop
the direction toward darkness if they choose to do so, which
they do not," says Joe. "One of my jobs in that point in the
story is to create a sense in the viewer's mind that, as far as
the show's concerned, there's a madman at the wheel who
will do just about anything he wants to, and if that means
taking the car off the tracks and crashing it, then that's what
we'll do."

The episode represents a major turning point for Londo.

The whole season was setting him up for a fall, with the underlying bitterness and pathos of the character leading him to accept Morden's offer to "fix" the Narn problem. His reaction when he finds out that fixing the problem meant the deaths of ten thousand Narns shows that he had no idea what he was getting into. "Then even when he sees it, he isn't able to look at the flash and the brilliance," says Peter Jurasik. "It intrigues him and blinds him, that flash of power. Even though consciously he's able to understand ten thousand—it comes out of his mouth—but it's not making an imprint on his brain because of the potency of the taste of power. I'm just a small-time actor playing a character in a science fiction show, so I don't know anything about this great power, but I guess it really is the ultimate intoxication."

His tempter, his serpent in the garden, is Morden. This was Ed Wasser's first episode in the role because, although the audience had already seen him in "Signs and Portents," "Chrysalis" was filmed first in order to give the production team enough time to finish the special effects. Ed believes that when Joe Straczynski wrote the part for him he saw Morden as lighter, more affable, and charming. "I don't think he expected dark, powerful energy," says Ed. "So when I finished my first day of shooting, at the end of the evening, I went to his office and said, 'What do you think?' He said, 'Well, it's not what I was expecting. I think you overworked the character. It's not you. I wanted you. I wrote the part for you, your energy, your lightness, your agility.' I felt really bad, and I left with my tail between my legs, thinking, 'I suck. I blew it.' And Joe—which says a lot about Joe—called me the very next day and said, 'I just want you to know, we took a look at the dailies, and they're really terrific and it's going to make for a great show, so congratulations.' "

The actions of Morden's associates reignite the ancient conflict between the Narn and Centauri, completely turning the tables on the situation that had been presented in "Midnight on the Firing Line." It makes the Centauri the aggressors and the Narn the victims. The contrast between G'Kar's vibrant, warlike tirades of the first episode and the emotion when Na'Toth tells him about the destruction in Quadrant 37 demonstrates how the audience's perceptions have been turned full circle.

"We were so emotional the first take that our director said, 'You guys are almost crying. You can't, too much, back off,' " remembers Julie Caitlin Brown, who plays Na'Toth. "He took my hand in the first take, and it so moved me. He said, 'You were so full of emotion that my instinct was to comfort you by taking your hand.' And the minute he touched me, tears welled up in my eyes. You can imagine with big red lenses what that looked like. She [Janet Greek, the director] said, 'Know that that's there, but don't let it come up.' "

While conflict between the Narns and Centauri threatens the peace of the galaxy as a whole, internal matters on Earth signal an upheaval for Humanity. All the political problems laid down in the earlier part of the season culminate in this episode, in which Babylon 5 finds itself caught up in the plot to assassinate President Santiago and is powerless to stop it. "As someone who lived through the Kennedy assassination, my job there was to try and evoke a similar feeling, if I could possibly do so," says Joe Straczynski. "I think that it succeeded fairly well in creating a feeling of real dread and loss. Oddly enough, the scene we shot where Clark is sworn in on EarthForce Two, we staged that using actual photographs from when Lyndon Johnson was sworn in following the assassination of John F. Kennedy. And by the universe of strange coincidence, we ended up shooting it on the day of that anniversary. So it was a very strange atmosphere on the set that day."

When Garibaldi is shot by conspirators to stop him from revealing what he knows about the assassination, it makes for one of the nicest visual moments of the episode. The scene goes into slow motion, the PPG blast flares against his back, his face contorts in pain, and he falls out of frame to reveal his aide holding a smoking gun. "That was a pretty easy one to do actually," says Janet Greek. "I just wanted to make it really mysterious and shocking. I know that it looks good, but it was really very simple to do."

Nevertheless, the events are quite dramatic for Garibaldi. As he fights unconsciousness to tell Sinclair the vital information that he has discovered, it increases the tension, leaving a sense of dread hanging over the scene. "There's ways that you can tweak yourself to make the performance a little more real," says Jerry Doyle. "If you hold your breath for a minute and a half, finally, when it comes time to say your line, you're like [gasping], 'They're going to kill . . .' because then you're *really* trying to get your breath."

At the same time, Delenn is preparing for something that will change her life forever. Her decision to enter the chrysalis was flagged on many occasions, in "Soul Hunter," "Parliament of Dreams," "Legacies," and "Babylon Squared," while in others she was seen building the structure where she finally places the triluminary in readiness for the transformation. The final moment when she entered the chrysalis was so important that it generated a great deal of discussion. "We couldn't all agree on what we wanted to see," says Janet Greek. "We couldn't agree on how big it should be— we couldn't really agree on anything. We didn't know how much of Delenn to reveal in there, how much not to. Through the preproduction and during the production, I was constantly going onto the set and looking at what they were doing with the latex and everything else. They built it, and then they put all that stuff over it—it's like cobwebs—and that really helped it."

What was going to happen to Delenn when—and if—she came out of the chrysalis was one of the many unresolved questions designed to keep viewers intrigued while waiting for the next season. There was also the new threat of Morden's "associates," who, we would later learn, are the Shadows. Garibaldi's life hung in the balance. And there was the question over what happened to Sinclair at the Battle of the Line, which was teased in "Chrysalis" but not answered. Even so, at the time the episode was made, there was no guarantee there would be a second season. "It was pure faith," says Joe Straczynski. "We never know at that stage in the game: we have to work on the assumption that it's going to happen. I figured, with this particular storyline, if we didn't get renewed, I imagined mobs storming the gate at Warner Bros., which would, at least, be some small revenge."

Fortunately, *Babylon 5* was renewed for another season, and all those questions came to be addressed in time.

But that is another story.

CPSIA information can be obtained
at www.ICGtesting.com
Printed in the USA
LVHW112342031122
732308LV00002B/355